# THE SHERLOCK HOLMES ADVENTURES!

Adapted for Younger Readers by
THOMAS SEWELL

from the tales of
SIR ARTHUR CONAN DOYLE

**A Rising Star Visionary Press book**
**for extra copies please contact by e-mail at**
**risingstarvisionarypress@earthlink.net**
**or send by regular mail to**
**Rising Star Visionary Press**
**Copies Department**
**P O Box 9226**
**Fountain Valley, CA 92728-9226**

http://www.risingstarvisionarypress.vpweb.com/

# Adapting Sherlock Holmes

When Charles, my nine-year-old son, saw the first previews for the new Robert Downey, Jr. *Sherlock Holmes* movie, he grew quite excited. After all, if Iron Man chose a 19th century British detective as his next big role, it's *gotta* be new and interesting, right?

So you can only imagine how surprised he was when I revealed that Downey, Jr.'s *Holmes* was far from new; that the character of Sherlock Holmes had, in fact, already appeared in some 200+ movies!

This led to a whole onslaught of questions, as only a nine-year-old can fire away! I considered renting one of the Basil Rathbone or Frank Langella versions, but decided that it might be better to enhance his literary experience and go back to the Sir Arthur Conan Doyle originals.

(After all, his old man's meager short-story awards did not impress, but a character graced by Iron Man himself was another matter altogether!)

So I downloaded a copy of *The Adventures of Sherlock Holmes* to my Amazon Kindle and sat down to read them together ...

... and thank heaven that I did!

Granted, it had been many, many years since I read any of Doyle's original works in college, but I was still shocked to find the great Sherlock Holmes ... *lost in a haze of **cocaine***???

I quickly opted to read the rest of the stories

myself first, but sure enough: Holmes doing cocaine! Holmes in an opium den!  And we all know the famous image of Holmes and his pipe, but I hadn't realized just how much the detective indulged the habit, treating smoking not just as a vice but as practically necessary to his thinking process?!  And they say that *video games* are a bad influence on our children!

So I talked it over with Charles' mother and we decided to write a few query emails and contact a few old friends in the publishing business ... and, thanks to my old mentor Daniel and his daughter Lindsey at Rising Star Visionary Press (not to mention the fact that *Sherlock Holmes* is now public domain!), I now present to you *The Sherlock Holmes Adventures!*, adapted for young readers!

I will admit, the bulk of what follows is still Doyle's original work—the vast majority of it, in fact.  But gone are the references to Holmes' callous abuse of his temple—in fact, the only story that still contains drug references (an opium den) remains because the context highlights the drug's destructive potential, as it should be!

And while I was at it, I made some other minor tweaks as well.  I didn't want my son telling his school buddies about Holmes and quoting such now-unwholesome words as "ejaculated," "fagged," and so on—they may have had different meaning back in Doyle's day, but I'd rather steer clear of the Principal's office, thank you very much!

Other small alterations include changing "pray" when the characters meant "please," identifying "pince-nez" as spectacles, combining "to-night" into "tonight," etc., etc.

So I present to you, Caring Parents, a version of six of Sherlock Holmes' adventures that you can allow your youngsters to read without fear!  This is the longest project I have worked on—short-stories are generally my bread and butter.  But since this work is a *collection of short-stories*, I felt reasonably at home.

God bless you all!

Thomas Sewell

# TABLE OF CONTENTS

# 1<sup>st</sup> ADVENTURE!
## A SCANDAL IN BOHEMIA

### I

To my friend Sherlock Holmes, she is always "the woman."

I have seldom heard him mention her under any other name. In his eyes, she eclipses and predominates the whole of her gender. It was not that he felt any emotion akin to "love" for Irene Adler—all emotions, and that one in particular, were repulsive to his cold, precise but admirably balanced mind. He was the most perfect reasoning and observing machine that the world has seen ... but as a lover, he would have placed himself in a false position. He never spoke of the softer passions, except with sarcasm and a sneer. They were admirable things for the observer—excellent for exposing men's motives and actions. But for the trained reasoner to admit such intrusions into his own delicate and finely-adjusted temperament was to introduce a distracting factor which might throw a doubt over all his mental accomplishments. Dust in a sensitive instrument, or a crack in one of his own high-power lenses, would not be more disturbing than a strong emotion in a nature such as his. And yet there was but one woman to him, and that woman was the late Irene Adler, of problematic and questionable memory.

I had seen little of Holmes lately. My marriage had drifted us away from each other. My own complete happiness, and the home-centered interests which rise up around the man who first finds himself master of his own establishment, were sufficient to absorb all my attention ... while Holmes, who loathed every form of society with his whole go-as-you-please soul, remained in our lodgings in Baker Street, buried among his old books. He was still, as ever, deeply attracted by the study of crime, and occupied his immense faculties and extraordinary powers of observation in examining those clues, and clearing up those mysteries which had been abandoned as "hopeless" by the official police. From time to time, I heard some vague account of his doings—of his summons to Odessa in the case of the Trepoff murder; of his clearing up of the singular tragedy of the Atkinson brothers at Trincomalee; and, finally, of the mission which he had accomplished so delicately and successfully for the reigning family of Holland. Beyond these signs of his activity, however, which I merely shared with all the readers of the daily press, I knew little of my former friend and companion.

One night—it was on the 20th of March, 1888—I was returning from a journey to a patient (I had now returned to civil practice), when my way led me through Baker Street. As I passed the well-remembered door, I was seized with a keen desire to see Holmes again, and to know how he was using his extraordinary powers. His rooms were brilliantly lit, and—even as I looked up—I saw his tall, slender figure pass twice in a dark silhouette against the blind. He was pacing the room swiftly, eagerly, with his head down and his hands clasped behind him.

To me, who knew his every mood and habit, his attitude and manner told their own story. He was at work again, hot upon the scent of some new problem. I rang the bell and was shown up to the chamber which had formerly been in part my own.

His manner was reserved—it always was; but he was glad, I think, to see me. With hardly a word spoken, but with a kind expression, he waved me to an armchair, then he stood before the fire and looked me over in his singular introspective fashion.

"Wedlock suits you," he remarked. "I think, Watson, that you have put on seven and a half pounds since I saw you."

"Seven!" I answered.

"Indeed, I should have thought a little more. Just a little more, I imagine, Watson. And in practice again, I observe. You did not tell me that you intended to go back to work."

"Then, how do you know?"

"I see it, I deduce it. How do I know that you have been getting yourself very wet lately, and that you have a most clumsy and careless servant girl?"

"My dear Holmes," I said, "this is too much! You would certainly have been burned at the stake, had you lived a few centuries ago. It is true that I had a country walk on Thursday and came home in a dreadful mess, but as I have changed my clothes I can't imagine how you deduce it. As to Mary Jane, she is disobedient, and my wife has given her notice … but again, I fail to see how you work it out."

He chuckled to himself and rubbed his hands together.

"It is simplicity itself!" he said. "My eyes tell me that on the inside of your left shoe, just where the firelight strikes it, the leather is damaged by six almost parallel cuts. Obviously, they have been caused by someone who has very carelessly scraped round the edges of the sole in order to remove crusted mud from it. Hence, you see, my double deduction that you had been out in vile weather, and that you had a particularly malignant boot-slitting specimen of the London workforce. As to your practice, if a gentleman walks into my rooms smelling of medicine, with a black mark of nitrate-of-silver upon his right forefinger, and a bulge on the right side of his top-hat to show where he has secreted his stethoscope, I must be dull, indeed, if I do not pronounce him to be an active member of the medical profession."

I could not help laughing at the ease with which he explained his process of deduction. "When I hear you give your reasons," I remarked, "it always appears to me to be so ridiculously simple that I could easily do it myself, though at each following example of your reasoning I am baffled until you explain your process! And yet, I believe that my eyes are as good as yours."

"Quite so," he answered, throwing himself down into an armchair. "You see, but you do not observe. The distinction is clear. For example, you have frequently seen the steps which lead up from the hall to this room?"

"Frequently."

"How often?"

"Well, several hundred times!"

"Then how many are there?"

"How many? I don't know."

"Quite so! You have not observed. And yet you have seen. That is just my point! Now, I know that there are seventeen steps, because I have both seen and observed.  By the way, since you are interested in these little problems, and since you are good enough to write a journal of one or two of my trivial experiences, you may be interested in this."  He threw over a sheet of thick, pink-tinted note-paper which had been lying open upon the table.  "It came by the last post," he said.  "Read it aloud."

The note was undated, and without either signature or address.

" 'There will call upon you tonight, at a quarter to eight o'clock, a gentleman who desires to consult you upon a matter of the very deepest importance.  Your recent services to one of the royal houses of Europe have shown that you are one who may safely be trusted with matters which are of an importance, which can hardly be exaggerated.  This account of you we have from all quarters received.  Be in your chamber at that hour, and do not take it amiss if your visitor wears a mask.'

"This is indeed a mystery," I remarked.  "What do you imagine that it means?"

"I have no data yet—it is a mistake to theorize before one has data.  One inevitably begins to twist facts to suit theories, instead of theories to suit facts.  But the note itself ... what do you deduce from it?"

I carefully examined the writing, and the paper upon which it was written.

"The man who wrote it was presumably well to do," I remarked, endeavoring to imitate my companion's processes.  "Such paper could not be bought under half a crown a packet.  It is peculiarly strong and stiff."

"Peculiar—*that* is the very word," said Holmes.  "It is not an English paper at all.  Hold it up to the light."

I did so, and saw a large "E" with a small "g," a

"P," and a large "G" with a small "t" woven into the texture of the paper.

"What do you make of that?" asked Holmes.

"The name of the maker, no doubt; or his monogram, rather."

"Not at all.  The 'G' with the small 't' stands for 'Gesellschaft,' which is German for 'Company.'  It is a customary contraction like our 'Co.'  'P,' of course, stands for 'Papier.'  Now for the 'Eg.'  Let us glance at our Continental Gazetteer." He took down a heavy brown volume from his shelves. "Eglow, Eglonitz—here we are, Egria.  It is in a German-speaking country— in Bohemia, not far from Carlsbad. 'Remarkable as being the scene of the death of Wallenstein, and for its numerous glass-factories and paper-mills.'  Ha, ha, my boy, what do you make of that?"  His eyes sparkled.

"The paper was made in Bohemia," I said.

"Precisely.  And the man who wrote the note is German.  Do you note the peculiar construction of the sentence—'This account of you we have from all quarters received.'  A Frenchman or Russian could not have written that.  It is the German who is so improper with his verbs.  It only remains, therefore, to discover what is wanted by this German who writes upon Bohemian paper and prefers wearing a mask to showing his face.  And here he comes, if I am not mistaken, to answer all our questions."

As he spoke there was the sharp sound of horses' hoofs and grating wheels against the curb, followed by a sharp pull at the bell. Holmes whistled.

"A pair, by the sound," he said.  "Yes," he continued, glancing out of the window.  "A nice little brougham and a pair of beauties. A hundred and fifty guineas apiece.   There's money in this case,

Watson, if there is nothing else."

"I think that I had better go, Holmes."

"Not a bit, Doctor. Stay where you are. I have missed your company. And this promises to be interesting. It would be a pity to miss it!"

"But your client—"

"Never mind him. I may want your help, and so may he. Here he comes. Sit down in that armchair, Doctor, and give us your best attention!"

A slow and heavy step, which had been heard upon the stairs and in the passage, paused immediately outside the door. Then there was a loud and authoritative tap.

"Come in!" said Holmes.

A man entered who could hardly have been less than six feet six inches in height, with the chest and limbs of a Hercules. His dress was rich with a richness which would, in England, be looked upon as akin to bad taste. Heavy bands of astrakhan were slashed across the sleeves and fronts of his double-breasted coat, while the deep blue cloak which was thrown over his shoulders was lined with flame-colored silk and secured at the neck with a brooch which consisted of a single flaming beryl. Boots which extended halfway up his calves, and which were trimmed at the tops with rich brown fur, completed the impression of barbaric luxury which was suggested by his whole appearance. He carried a broad-brimmed hat in his hand, while he wore across the upper part of his face, extending down past the cheekbones, a black vizard mask, which he had apparently adjusted that very moment, for his hand was still raised to it as he entered. From the lower part of the face he appeared to be a man of strong character, with a thick, hanging lip, and a long, straight chin suggestive of resolution pushed to the length of stubbornness.

"You had my note?" he asked with a deep harsh voice and a strongly marked German accent. "I told you that I would call." He looked from one to the other of us, as if uncertain which to address.

"Please take a seat," said Holmes. "This is my friend and colleague, Dr. Watson, who is occasionally good enough to help me in my cases. Whom have I the honor to address?"

"You may address me as the Count Von Kramm, a Bohemian nobleman. I understand that this gentleman, your friend, is a man of honor and discretion, whom I may trust with a matter of the most extreme importance. If not, I should much prefer to communicate with you alone."

I rose to go, but Holmes caught me by the wrist and pushed me back into my chair. "It is both, or none," he said. "You may say before this gentleman anything which you may say to me."

The Count shrugged his broad shoulders. "Then I must begin," he said, "by binding you both to absolute secrecy for two years; at the end of that time, the matter will be of no importance. At present, it is not too much to say that it is of such weight it may have an influence upon European history."

"I promise," said Holmes.

"And I."

"You will excuse this mask," continued our strange visitor. "The August person who employs me wishes his agent to be unknown to you, and I may confess at once that the title by which I have just called myself is not exactly my own."

"I was aware of it," said Holmes dryly.

"The circumstances are of great delicacy, and

every precaution has to be taken to quench what might grow to be an immense scandal and seriously compromise one of the reigning families of Europe. To speak plainly, the matter implicates the great House of Ormstein, hereditary kings of Bohemia."

"I was also aware of that," murmured Holmes, settling himself down in his armchair and closing his eyes.

Our visitor glanced with some apparent surprise at the languid, lounging figure of the man who had been no doubt depicted to him as the sharpest reasoner and most energetic agent in Europe. Holmes slowly reopened his eyes and looked impatiently at his gigantic client.

"If your Majesty would condescend to state your case," he remarked, "I should be better able to advise you."

The man sprang from his chair and paced up and down the room in uncontrollable agitation. Then, with a gesture of desperation, he tore the mask from his face and hurled it upon the ground. "You are right," he cried; "I am the King. Why should I attempt to conceal it?"

"Why, indeed?" murmured Holmes. "Your Majesty had not spoken before I was aware that I was addressing Wilhelm Gottsreich Sigismond von Ormstein, Grand Duke of Cassel-Felstein, and hereditary King of Bohemia."

"But you can understand," said our strange visitor, sitting down once more and passing his hand over his high white forehead, "that I am not accustomed to doing such business in my own person. Yet the matter was so delicate that I could not confide it to an agent without putting myself in his power. I have come in secret from Prague for the purpose of consulting you."

"Then, please—consult!" said Holmes, shutting his eyes once more.

"The facts are briefly these:  Some five years ago, during a lengthy visit to Warsaw, I made the acquaintance of the well-known adventuress, Irene Adler.  The name is no doubt familiar to you."

"Kindly look her up in my index, Doctor," murmured Holmes without opening his eyes.  For many years he had adopted a system of docketing all paragraphs concerning men and things, so that it was difficult to name a subject or a person on which he could not at once furnish information.  In this case, I found her biography sandwiched in between that of a Hebrew rabbi and that of a staff-commander who had written a monograph upon the deep-sea fishes.

"Let me see!" said Holmes. "Hmm! Born in New Jersey in the year 1858. Contralto—hmm! La Scala, hmm! Prima donna Imperial Opera of Warsaw—yes! Retired from operatic stage—ha!  Living in London—quite so!  Your Majesty, as I understand, became entangled with this young person, wrote her some compromising letters, and is now desirous of getting those letters back."

"Precisely so.  But how—?"

"Was there a secret marriage?"

"None."

"No legal papers or certificates?"

"None."

"Then I fail to follow your Majesty.  If this young person should produce her letters for blackmailing or other purposes, how is she to prove their authenticity?"

"There is the writing."

"Pooh, pooh!  Forgery."

"My private note-paper."

"Stolen!"

"My own seal."

"Imitated."

"My photograph."

"Bought."

"We were both in the photograph."

"Oh, dear! *That* is very bad! Your Majesty has indeed committed an indiscretion."

"I was mad—insane!"

"You have compromised yourself seriously."

"I was only Crown Prince then. I was young. I am only thirty now."

"It must be recovered."

"We have tried and failed."

"Your Majesty must pay. It must be bought."

"She will not sell."

"Stolen, then."

"Five attempts have been made! Twice burglars in my pay ransacked her house. Once we diverted her luggage when she traveled. Twice she has been waylaid. There has been no result!"

"No sign of it?"

"Absolutely none."

Holmes laughed. "It is quite a pretty little problem!"

"But a very serious one to me," returned the King reproachfully.

"Very, indeed. And what does she propose to do with the photograph?"

"To ruin me."

"But how?"

"I am about to be married."

"So I have heard."

"To Clotilde Lothman von Saxe-Meningen,

second daughter of the King of Scandinavia.  You may know the strict principles of her family.  She is herself the very soul of delicacy.  A shadow of a doubt as to my conduct would bring the matter to an end."

"And Irene Adler?"

"Threatens to send them the photograph.  And she will do it.  I know that she will do it!  You do not know her, but she has a soul of steel.  She has the face of the most beautiful of women, and the mind of the most resolute of men.  Rather than I should marry another woman, there are no lengths to which she would not go—none!"

"You are sure that she has not sent it yet?"

"I am sure."

"And why?"

"Because she has said that she would send it on the day when the betrothal was publicly proclaimed.  That will be next Monday."

"Oh, then we have three days yet," said Holmes with a yawn.  "That is very fortunate, as I have one or two matters of importance to look into just at present.  Your Majesty will, of course, stay in London for the present?"

"Certainly.  You will find me at the Langham under the name of the Count Von Kramm."

"Then I shall drop you a line to let you know how we progress."

"Please do so.  I shall be all anxiety."

"Then, as to money?"

"You have a blank check."

"Absolutely?"

"I tell you that I would give one of the provinces of my kingdom to have that photograph."

"And for present expenses?"

The King took a heavy chamois leather bag from under his cloak and laid it on the table.  "There are three hundred pounds in gold and seven hundred in notes."

Holmes scribbled a receipt upon a sheet of his notebook and handed it to him.

"And Mademoiselle's address?" he asked.

"Is Briony Lodge, Serpentine Avenue, St.  John's Wood."

Holmes took a note of it.  "One other question.  Was the photograph cabinet-size?"

"It was."

"Then, goodnight, your Majesty, and I trust that we shall soon have some good news for you."

"And goodnight, Watson," he soon added, as the wheels of the royal brougham rolled down the street.  "If you will be good enough to call tomorrow afternoon at three o'clock, I should like to chat this little matter over with you."

## II

At three o'clock precisely, I was at Baker Street, but Holmes had not yet returned.  The landlady informed me that he had left the house shortly after eight o'clock in the morning.

I sat down beside the fire with the intention of awaiting him, however long he might be.  I was already deeply interested in his inquiry, for, though it was surrounded by none of the grim and strange features associated with the crimes which I have already recorded, the nature of the case and the exalted station of his client gave it a character of its own.  Indeed, apart from the nature of the investigation which my friend had on hand, there was something in his masterly grasp of a situation, and his keen, sharp reasoning, which made it a pleasure to me to study his system of work and to follow the quick, subtle methods by which he disentangled the most inextricable mysteries. I was so accustomed to his invariable success that the very possibility of his failing had ceased to enter into my mind!

It was close upon to four o'clock before the door opened, and a drunken-looking stableman—ill-kempt and side-whiskered—with an inflamed face and disreputable clothes, walked into the room. Accustomed as I was to my friend's amazing powers of disguise, I had to look three times before I was certain that it was indeed him! With a nod, he vanished into the bedroom, then emerged in five minutes—tweed-suited and respectable, as always. Putting his hands into his pockets, he stretched out his legs in front of the fire and laughed heartily for some minutes.

"Well, really!" he cried, and then he choked and laughed again until he was obliged to lie back, limp and helpless, in the chair.

"What is it?"

"It's quite too funny. I am sure you could never guess how I employed my morning, or what I ended up doing."

"I can't imagine. I suppose that you have been watching the habits, and perhaps the house, of Miss Irene Adler."

"Quite so; but the sequel was rather unusual. I will tell you, however.

"I left the house a little after eight o'clock this morning in the character of an out-of-work stableman. There is a wonderful sympathy and comradery among horsey men. Be one of them, and you will know all that there is to know. I soon found

Briony Lodge.  It is a feminine villa, with a garden at the back, but built out in front right up to the road, two stories.  Charming look to the door, large sitting-room on the right side, well-furnished, with long windows almost to the floor, and those preposterous English window fasteners which a child could open.  Behind there was nothing remarkable, except that the passage window could be reached from the top of the coach-house.  I walked round it and examined it closely from every point of view, but without noting anything else of interest.

"I then lounged down the street and found, as I expected, that there was a stable house in a lane which runs down by one wall of the garden.  I lent the workers a hand in rubbing down their horses, and received in exchange twopence, a glass of half-and-half, two fills of tobacco, and as much information as I could desire about Miss Adler, to say nothing of a half-dozen other people in the neighborhood in whom I was not in the least interested, but to whose biographies I was compelled to listen."

"And what of Irene Adler?" I asked.

"Oh, she has turned all the men's heads.  She is the daintiest thing under a bonnet on this planet.  She lives quietly, sings at concerts, drives out at five every day, and returns at seven sharp for dinner.  Seldom goes out at other times, except when she sings.  Has only one male visitor—he is dark, handsome, and dashing, never calls less than once a day, and often twice.  He is one Mr. Godfrey Norton, of the Inner Temple.  See the advantages of a cabman as a confidant!  When I had listened to all they had to tell, I began to walk up and down near Briony Lodge once more, and to think over my plan.

"This Godfrey Norton was evidently an important

factor in the matter. He was a lawyer—that sounded ominous! What was the relation between them, and what was the object of his repeated visits? Was she his client, his friend, or his mistress? If the former, she had probably transferred the photograph to his keeping. If the latter, it was less likely. On the issue of this question depended whether I should continue my work at Briony Lodge, or turn my attention to the gentleman's chambers in the Temple. It was a delicate point, and it widened the field of my inquiry. I fear that I bore you with these details, but I have to let you see my little difficulties, if you are to understand the situation."

"I am following you closely," I answered.

"I was still balancing the matter in my mind when a hansom cab drove up to Briony Lodge, and a gentleman sprang out. He was a remarkably handsome man, dark and moustached—evidently the man of whom I had heard. He appeared to be in a great hurry, shouted to the cabman to wait, and brushed past the maid who opened the door with the air of a man who was thoroughly at home.

"He was in the house about half an hour, and I could catch glimpses of him in the windows of the sitting-room, pacing up and down, talking excitedly, and waving his arms. Of her I could see nothing. Presently he emerged, looking even more flurried than before. As he stepped up to the cab, he pulled a gold watch from his pocket and looked at it earnestly, 'Drive like the devil,' he shouted, 'first to Gross & Hankey's in Regent Street, and then to the Church of St. Monica in the Edgeware Road. Half a guinea if you do it in twenty minutes!'

"Away they went, and I was just wondering whether I should not do well to follow them when up the lane came a neat little horse-drawn carriage, the coachman with his coat only half-buttoned, and his tie under his ear, while all the tags of his harness were sticking out of the buckles.  It hadn't pulled up before she shot out of the hall door and into it.  I only caught a glimpse of her at the moment, but she was a lovely woman, with a face that a man might die for.

"'The Church of St.  Monica, John,' she cried, 'and half a sovereign if you reach it in twenty minutes.'

"This was quite too good to lose, Watson.  I was just balancing whether I should run for it, or whether I should perch behind her carriage when a cab came through the street.  The driver looked twice at such a shabby fare, but I jumped in before he could object. 'The Church of St.  Monica,' said I, 'and half a sovereign if you reach it in twenty minutes.'  It was twenty-five minutes to twelve, and of course it was clear enough what was in the wind.

"My cabby drove fast.  I don't think I ever drove faster, but the others were there before us.  The cab and the carriage with their steaming horses were in front of the door when I arrived.  I paid the man and hurried into the church.  There was not a soul there save the two whom I had followed and a clergyman, who seemed to be conversing with them.  They were all three standing in a knot in front of the altar.  I lounged up the side aisle like any other idler who has dropped into a church. Suddenly, to my surprise, the three at the altar faced round to me, and Godfrey Norton came running as hard as he could towards me.

"'Thank God,' he cried.  'You'll do.  Come!  Come!'

"'What then?' I asked.

"'Come, man, come, only three minutes, or it won't be legal.'

"I was half-dragged up to the altar, and before I knew where I was, I found myself mumbling responses which were whispered in my ear, and vouching for things of which I knew nothing, and generally assisting in the secure marrying of Irene Adler, spinster, to Godfrey Norton, bachelor. It was all done in an instant, and there was the gentleman thanking me on the one side and the lady on the other, while the clergyman beamed on me in front. It was the most preposterous position in which I ever found myself in my life! And it was the thought of it that started me laughing just now. It seems that there had been some informality about their license, that the clergyman absolutely refused to marry them without a witness of some sort, and that my lucky appearance saved the bridegroom from having to rush out into the streets in search of a best man. The bride gave me a sovereign, and I mean to wear it on my watch-chain in memory of the occasion."

"This is a very unexpected turn of affairs!" I exclaimed. "And what then?"

"Well, I found my plans very seriously menaced. It looked as if the pair might take an immediate departure, and so necessitate very prompt and energetic measures on my part. At the church door, however, they separated, he driving back to the Temple, and she to her own house. 'I shall drive out in the park at five as usual,' she said as she left him. I heard no more. They drove away in different directions, and I went off to make my own arrangements."

"Which are?"

"Some cold beef and a glass of beer," he

answered, ringing the bell. "I have been too busy to think of food, and I am likely to be busier still this evening.  By the way, Doctor, I shall want your cooperation."

"I shall be delighted."

"You don't mind breaking the law?"

"Not in the least."

"Nor running a chance of arrest?"

"Not in a good cause."

"Oh, the cause is excellent!"

"Then I am your man!"

"I was sure that I might rely on you."

"But what is it you wish?"

"When Mrs. Turner has brought in the tray, I will make it clear to you.  Now," he said as he turned hungrily on the simple fare that our landlady had provided, "I must discuss it while I eat, for I don't have much time—it is nearly five now.  In two hours we must be on the scene of action.  Miss Irene—or Madame, rather—returns from her drive at seven.  We must be at Briony Lodge to meet her."

"And what then?"

"You must leave that to me.  I have already arranged what is to occur.  There is only one point on which I must insist.  You must *not* interfere, come what may!  You understand?"

"I am to be neutral?"

"To do nothing whatever!  There will probably be some small unpleasantness.  Do not join in it.  It will end in my being conveyed into the house.  Four or five minutes afterwards, the sitting-room window will open.  You are to station yourself close to that open window."

"Yes."

"You are to watch me, for I will be visible to you."

"Yes."

"And when I raise my hand—like this—you will throw into the room what I give you to throw, and will, at the same time, raise the cry of fire. You quite follow me?"

"Entirely."

"It is nothing very formidable," he said, taking a long cigar-shaped roll from his pocket. "It is an ordinary plumber's smoke-rocket, fitted with a cap at either end to make it self-lighting. Your task is confined to that. When you raise your cry of fire, it will be taken up by quite a number of people. You may then walk to the end of the street, and I will rejoin you in ten minutes. I hope that I have made myself clear?"

"I am to remain neutral, to get near the window, to watch you, and at the signal to throw in this object, then to raise the cry of fire, and to wait for you at the corner of the street."

"Precisely."

"Then you may entirely rely on me!"

"That is excellent. I think, perhaps, it is almost time that I prepare for the new role I have to play."

He disappeared into his bedroom and returned in a few minutes in the character of an amiable and simple-minded Nonconformist clergyman. His broad black hat, his baggy trousers, his white tie, his sympathetic smile ... It was not merely that Holmes changed his costume—his expression, his manner, his very soul seemed to vary with every fresh part that he assumed!  The stage lost a fine actor, even as science lost an acute reasoner, when he became a specialist in crime.

It was a quarter past six when we left Baker Street, and it still wanted ten minutes to the hour when we found ourselves in Serpentine Avenue. It was already dusk, and the lamps were just being lighted as we paced up and down in front of Briony Lodge, waiting for the coming of its occupant. The house was just as Holmes had described, but the locality appeared to be less private than I expected—on the contrary, for a small street in a quiet neighborhood, it was remarkably active. There was a group of shabbily dressed men smoking and laughing in a corner, a scissors-grinder with his wheel, two guardsmen who were flirting with a nurse, and several well-dressed young men who were lounging up and down with cigars in their mouths.

"You see," remarked Holmes, as we paced to and fro in front of the house, "this marriage rather simplifies matters. The photograph becomes a double-edged weapon now. The chances are that she would be just as averse to its being seen by Mr. Godfrey Norton as *our client* is to its coming to the eyes of his princess. Now the question is: Where are we to find the photograph?"

"Where, indeed?"

"It is most unlikely that she carries it about with her. It is cabinet-size—too large for easy concealment within a woman's dress. She knows that the King is capable of having her waylaid and searched. Two attempts of the sort have already been made. We may take it, then, that she does not carry it about with her."

"Where, then?"

"Her banker or her lawyer, there is that double possibility. But I am inclined to think neither. Women are naturally secretive, and they like to do their own secreting! Why should she hand it over to anyone else? She could trust her own guardianship, but she could not tell what indirect or political influence might be brought to bear upon a business man. Besides, remember that she had resolved to use it within a few days. It must be where she can lay her hands upon it. It must be in her own house."

"But it has twice been burgled."

"Pshaw! They did not know how to look."

"But how will you look?"

"I will not look."

"What then?"

"I will get her to show me."

"But she will refuse."

"She will not be able to. But I hear the rumble of wheels—it is her carriage! Now carry out my orders to the letter."

As he spoke, the gleam of the side-lights of a carriage came round the curve of the avenue. It was a smart little landau which rattled up to the door of Briony Lodge. As it pulled up, one of the loafing men at the corner dashed forward to open the door in the hope of earning a copper, but was elbowed away by another loafer, who had rushed up with the same intention. A fierce quarrel broke out, which was increased by the two guardsmen, who took sides with one of the loungers, and by the scissors-grinder, who was equally hot upon the other side. A blow was struck, and in an instant the lady, who had stepped from her carriage, was the center of a little knot of flushed and struggling men, who struck savagely at each other with their fists and sticks.

Holmes dashed into the crowd to protect the lady, but just as he reached her he gave a cry and dropped to the ground, with the blood running freely down his face! When he fell, the guardsmen took to their heels in one direction and the loungers in the other, while a number of better-dressed people, who had watched the scuffle without taking part in it, crowded in to help the lady and to attend to the injured man. Irene Adler, as I will still call her, had hurried up the steps; but she stood at the top with her superb figure outlined against the lights of the hall, looking back into the street.

"Is the poor gentleman much hurt?" she asked.

"He is dead," cried several voices.

"No, no, there's life in him!" shouted another. "But he'll be gone before you can get him to hospital."

"He's a brave fellow," said a woman. "They would have had the lady's purse and watch if it hadn't been for him. They were a gang, and a rough one, too. Ah, he's breathing now."

"He can't lie in the street. May we bring him in, ma'am?"

"Surely. Bring him into the sitting-room. There is a comfortable sofa. This way, please!"

Slowly and solemnly, Holmes was borne into Briony Lodge and laid out in the principal room, while I still observed the proceedings from my post by the window. The lamps had been lit, but the blinds had not been drawn, so that I could see Holmes as he lay upon the couch. I do not know whether he was seized with compunction at that moment for the part he was playing, but I know that I never felt more heartily ashamed of myself in my life than when I saw the beautiful creature against whom I was conspiring, or the grace and kindliness with which she waited upon the injured man. And yet it would be the blackest treachery to Holmes to draw back now from the part which he had intrusted to me.

I hardened my heart, and took the smoke-rocket from under my ulster. After all, I thought, we are not injuring her—we were preventing her from injuring another!

Holmes had sat up upon the couch, and I saw him motion like a man who is in need of air. A maid rushed across and threw open the window. At the same instant I saw him raise his hand and at the signal, I tossed my rocket into the room with a cry of "Fire!" The word was no sooner out of my mouth than the whole crowd of spectators, well dressed and ill—gentlemen, ostlers, and servant-maids—joined in a general shriek of "Fire!"

Thick clouds of smoke curled through the room and out at the open window. I caught a glimpse of rushing figures, and a moment later the voice of Holmes from within assuring them that it was a false alarm.

Slipping through the shouting crowd, I made my way to the corner of the street, and in ten minutes was rejoiced to find my friend's arm in mine, and to get away from the scene of uproar. He walked swiftly and in silence for some few minutes until we had turned down one of the quiet streets which lead towards the Edgeware Road.

"You did it very nicely, Doctor," he remarked. "Nothing could have been better. It is all right."

"You have the photograph?"

"I know where it is."

"And how did you find out?"

"She showed me, as I told you she would."

"I am still in the dark."

"I do not wish to make a mystery," he said, laughing. "The matter was perfectly simple. You, of course, saw that everyone in the street was an accomplice. They were all engaged for the evening."

"I guessed as much."

"Then, when the row broke out, I had a little moist red paint in the palm of my hand. I rushed forward, fell down, clapped my hand to my face, and became a piteous spectacle. It is an old trick."

"That I also concluded."

"Then they carried me in. She was bound to have me in—what else could she do? And into her sitting-room, which was the very room which I suspected. It lay between that and her bedroom, and I was determined to see which. They laid me on a couch, I motioned for air, they were compelled to open the window, and you had your chance."

"How did that help you?"

"It was all-important. When a woman thinks that her house is on fire, her instinct is at once to rush to the thing which she values most—a married woman grabs at her baby; an unmarried one reaches for her jewel-box. It is a perfectly overpowering impulse, and I have more than once taken advantage of it. Now it was clear to me that our lady of today had nothing in the house more precious to her than what we are in quest of; she would rush to secure it. The alarm of fire was admirably done—the smoke and shouting were enough to shake nerves of steel! She responded beautifully. The photograph is in a recess behind a sliding panel just above the right bell-pull. She was there in an instant, and I caught a glimpse of it as she half-drew it out. When I cried out that it was a false alarm, she replaced it, glanced at the rocket, rushed from the room, and I have not seen her since. I rose, and, making my excuses, escaped from the house. I hesitated whether to attempt to secure the photograph at once; but the coachman had come in, and as he was watching me narrowly it seemed safer to wait. Impatience can ruin all!"

"And now?" I asked.

"Our quest is practically finished.  I shall call with the King tomorrow, and with you, if you care to come with us.  We will be shown into the sitting-room to wait for the lady, but it is probable that when she comes she may find neither us nor the photograph.  It might be a satisfaction to his Majesty to regain it with his own hands."

"And when will you call?"

"At eight in the morning.  She will not be up, so that we shall have a clear field. Besides, we must be prompt, for this marriage may mean a complete change in her life and habits.  I must wire to the King without delay!"

We had reached Baker Street and had stopped at the door.  He was searching his pockets for the key when someone passing said:

"Goodnight, Mr. Sherlock Holmes."

There were several people on the pavement at the time, but the greeting appeared to come from a slim youth in a heavy overcoat who had hurried by.

"I've heard that voice before," said Holmes, staring down the dimly lit street.  "Now, I wonder who the deuce that could have been."

III

I slept at Baker Street that night, and we were engaged upon our toast and coffee in the morning when the King of Bohemia rushed into the room.

"You have really got it?!" he cried, grasping Sherlock Holmes by either shoulder and looking eagerly into his face.

"Not yet."

"But you have hopes?"

"I have hopes."

"Then, come! I am all impatience to be gone."

"We must have a cab."

"No, my carriage is waiting."

"Then that will simplify matters." We descended and started off once more for Briony Lodge.

"Irene Adler is married," remarked Holmes.

"Married! When?"

"Yesterday."

"But to whom?"

"To an English lawyer named Norton."

"But she could not love him."

"I am in hopes that she does."

"And why in hopes?"

"Because it would spare your Majesty all fear of future annoyance. If the lady loves her husband, she does not love your Majesty. If she does not love your Majesty, there is no reason why she should interfere with your Majesty's plan."

"It is true. And yet—Well! I wish she had been of my own station! What a queen she would have made!" He relapsed into a moody silence, which was not broken until we drew up in Serpentine Avenue.

The door of Briony Lodge was open, and an elderly woman stood upon the steps. She watched us with a sardonic eye as we stepped from the carriage.

"Mr. Sherlock Holmes, I believe?" she asked.

"I am Mr. Holmes," answered my companion, looking at her with a questioning and rather startled gaze.

"Indeed! My mistress told me that you were likely to call. She left this morning with her husband by the 5:15 train from Charing Cross for the Continent."

"What?!" Sherlock Holmes staggered back, white with chagrin and surprise. "Do you mean that she has left England?"

"Never to return."

"And the papers?" asked the King hoarsely. "All is lost!"

"We shall see." Holmes pushed past the servant and rushed into the drawing-room, followed by the King and myself. The furniture was scattered about in every direction, with dismantled shelves and open drawers, as if the lady had hurriedly ransacked them before her flight. Holmes rushed at the bell-pull, tore back a small sliding shutter, and, plunging in his hand, pulled out a photograph and a letter. The photograph was of Irene Adler herself in evening dress, the letter was superscribed to "Sherlock Holmes, Esq. To be left till called for." My friend tore it open and we all three read it together. It was dated at midnight of the preceding night and ran in this way:

"MY DEAR MR. SHERLOCK HOLMES,

"You really did it very well. You took me in completely. Until after the alarm of fire, I had not a suspicion. But then, when I found how I had betrayed myself, I began to think. I had been warned against you months ago. I had been told that if the King employed an agent, it would certainly be you. And your address had been given me. Yet, with all this, you made me reveal what you wanted to know. Even after I became suspicious, I found it hard to think evil of such a dear, kind old clergyman. But, you know, I have been trained as an actress myself. Male costume is nothing new to me. I often take advantage of the freedom which it gives. I sent John, the coachman, to watch you, ran up stairs, got into my walking-clothes, as I call them, and came down just as you departed.

"Well, I followed you to your door, and so made sure that I was really an object of interest to the celebrated Mr. Sherlock Holmes.  Then I, rather carelessly, wished you goodnight, and started for the Temple to see my husband.

"We both thought the best resource was flight, when pursued by so formidable an antagonist; so you will find the nest empty when you call tomorrow.  As to the photograph, your client may rest in peace.  I love and am loved by a better man than he!  The King may do what he will without hindrance from one whom he has cruelly wronged.  I keep it only to safeguard myself, and to preserve a weapon which will always secure me from any steps which he might take in the future.  I leave a photograph which he might care to possess; and I remain, dear Mr. Sherlock Holmes,

"Very truly yours,

    "IRENE NORTON, née ADLER."


"What a woman—oh, what a woman!" cried the King of Bohemia, when we had all three read it.  "Did I not tell you how quick and resolute she was?  Would she not have made an admirable queen?  Is it not a pity that she was not on my level?"

"From what I have seen of the lady she seems indeed to be on a very different level to your Majesty," said Holmes coldly.  "I am sorry that I have not been able to bring your Majesty's business to a more successful conclusion."

"On the contrary, my dear sir!" cried the King.  "Nothing could be more successful!  I know that her word is inviolate.  The photograph is now as safe as if it were in the fire."

"I am glad to hear your Majesty say so."

"I am immensely indebted to you. Pray tell me in what way I can reward you. This ring—" He slipped an emerald snake ring from his finger and held it out upon the palm of his hand.

"Your Majesty has something which I should value even more highly," said Holmes.

"You have but to name it."

"This photograph!"

The King stared at him in amazement. "Irene's photograph? Certainly, if you wish it."

"I thank your Majesty. Then there is no more to be done in the matter. I have the honor to wish you a very good-morning." He bowed, and, turning away without observing the hand which the King had stretched out to him, he set off in my company for his chambers.

And that was how a great scandal threatened to affect the kingdom of Bohemia, and how the best plans of Mr. Sherlock Holmes were beaten by a woman's wit!

Holmes used to make merry over the cleverness of women, but I have not heard him do it of late. And when he speaks of Irene Adler, or when he refers to her photograph, it is always under the honorable title of "the woman!"

# 2<sup>nd</sup> ADVENTURE!
# THE RED-HEADED LEAGUE

I had called upon my friend, Mr. Sherlock Holmes, one day in the autumn of last year and found him in deep conversation with a very stout, flamboyant, elderly gentleman with fiery red hair. With an apology for my intrusion, I was about to withdraw when Holmes pulled me abruptly into the room and closed the door behind me.

"You could not possibly have come at a better time, my dear Watson," he said cordially.

"I was afraid that you were engaged."

"So I am.  Very much so."

"Then I can wait in the next room."

"Not at all."  Holmes turned back to the elderly man.  "This gentleman, Mr. Wilson, has been my partner and helper in many of my most successful cases, and I have no doubt that he will be of the utmost use to me in yours also."

The stout gentleman half rose from his chair and gave a bob of greeting, with a quick little questioning glance from his small fat-encircled eyes.

"Try the settee," said Holmes, relapsing into his armchair and putting his fingertips together, as was his custom when in judicial moods. "I know, my dear Watson, that you share my love of all that is bizarre and outside the conventions and humdrum routine of everyday life.  You have shown your relish for it by the enthusiasm which has prompted you to chronicle, and, if you will excuse my saying so, somewhat to *embellish* so many of my own little adventures."

"Your cases have indeed been of the greatest interest to me," I observed.

"You will remember that I remarked the other day that for strange effects and extraordinary combinations we must go to life itself, which is always far more daring than any effort of the imagination."

"A proposition which I took the liberty of doubting."

"You did, Doctor, but none the less you must come round to my view, for otherwise I shall keep on piling fact upon fact on you until your reason breaks down under them and acknowledges me to be right!" He smiled. "Now, Mr. Jabez Wilson here has been good enough to call upon me this morning, and to begin a narrative which promises to be one of the most singular which I have listened to for some time. You have heard me remark that the strangest and most unique things are very often connected not with the larger but with the smaller crimes, and occasionally, indeed, where there is room for doubt whether any positive crime has been committed. As far as I have heard, it is impossible for me to say whether the present case is an instance of crime or not, but the course of events is certainly among the most singular that I have ever listened to. Perhaps, Mr. Wilson, you would have the great kindness to recommence your narrative. I ask you not merely because my friend Dr. Watson has not heard the opening part, but also because the peculiar nature of the story makes me anxious to have every possible detail from your lips. As a rule, when I have heard some slight indication of the course of events, I am able to guide myself by the thousands of other similar cases which occur to my memory.  In the present instance, I am forced to admit that the facts are, to the best of my belief, unique."

The portly client puffed out his chest with an appearance of some little pride and pulled a dirty and wrinkled newspaper from the inside pocket of his greatcoat.  As he glanced down the advertisement column, with his head thrust forward and the paper flattened out upon his knee, I took a good look at the man and endeavored, after the fashion of my companion, to read the indications which might be presented by his dress or appearance.

I did not gain very much, however, by my inspection.  Our visitor bore every mark of being an average commonplace British tradesman, obese, pompous, and slow.  He wore rather baggy grey shepherd's check trousers, a not over-clean black frock-coat unbuttoned in the front, and a drab waistcoat with a heavy, brassy Albert chain, and a square, pierced bit of metal dangling down as an ornament.  A frayed top-hat and a faded brown overcoat with a wrinkled velvet collar lay upon a chair beside him.  Altogether, look as I would, there was nothing remarkable about the man save his blazing red head, and the expression of extreme chagrin and discontent upon his features.

Sherlock Holmes' quick eye took in my occupation, and he shook his head with a smile as he noticed my questioning glances.  "Beyond the obvious facts that he has at some time done manual labor, that he takes snuff, that he is a Freemason, that he has been in China, and that he has done a considerable amount of writing lately, I can deduce nothing else."

Mr. Jabez Wilson started up in his chair, with his forefinger upon the paper, but his eyes upon my companion.

"How, in the name of good-fortune, did you know all that, Mr. Holmes?" he asked. "How did you know, for example, that I did manual labor? It's as true as gospel, for I began as a ship's carpenter."

"Your hands, my dear sir. Your right hand is larger than your left. You have worked with it, and the muscles are more developed."

"Well, the snuff, then, and the Freemasonry?"

"I won't insult your intelligence by telling you how I read that, especially as, rather against the strict rules of your order, you use an arc-and-compass breastpin."

"Ah, of course, I forgot that. But the writing?"

"What else can be indicated by that right cuff so very shiny for five inches, and the left one with the smooth patch near the elbow where you rest it upon the desk?"

"Well, but China?"

"The fish that you have tattooed immediately above your right wrist could only have been done in China. I have made a small study of tattoo marks and have even contributed to the literature of the subject. That trick of staining the fishes' scales of a delicate pink is quite peculiar to China. When, in addition, I see a Chinese coin hanging from your watch-chain, the matter becomes even more simple."

Mr. Jabez Wilson laughed heavily. "Well, I never! I thought at first that you had done something clever, but I see that there was nothing in it, after all."

"I begin to think, Watson," said Holmes, "that I make a mistake in explaining. My poor little reputation, such as it is, will suffer shipwreck if I am so candid!  Can you not find the advertisement, Mr. Wilson?"

"Yes, I have got it now," he answered with his thick red finger planted halfway down the column.  "Here it is.  This is what began it all.  You just read it for yourself, sir."

I took the paper from him and read as follows:

"TO THE RED-HEADED LEAGUE:  On account of the bequest of the late Ezekiah Hopkins, of Lebanon, Pennsylvania, U.S.A., there is now another vacancy open which entitles a member of the League to a salary of 4 pounds a week for purely nominal services.  All red-headed men who are sound in body and mind and above the age of twenty-one years are eligible.  Apply in person on Monday, at eleven o'clock, to Duncan Ross, at the offices of the League, 7 Pope's Court, Fleet Street."

"What on earth does this mean?!" I cried after I had twice read over the extraordinary announcement.

Holmes chuckled and wriggled in his chair, as was his habit when in high spirits.  "It is a little off the beaten track, isn't it?" he said.  "And now, Mr. Wilson, tell us all about yourself, your household, and the effect which this advertisement had upon your fortunes.  You will first make a note, Doctor, of the paper and the date."

"It is The Morning Chronicle of April 27, 1890.  Just two months ago."

"Very good.  Now, Mr. Wilson?"

"Well, it is just as I have been telling you, Mr. Holmes," said Wilson, mopping his forehead.  "I have a small pawnbroker's business at Coburg Square, near the City.  It's not a very large affair, and of late years it has not done more than just give me a living. I used to be able to keep two assistants, but now I only keep one; and I would have a job to pay him but that he is willing to come for half wages so as to learn the business."

"What is the name of this obliging youth?" asked Sherlock Holmes.

"His name is Vincent Spaulding, and he's not such a youth, either.  It's hard to say his age.  I should not wish a smarter assistant, Mr. Holmes; and I know very well that he could better himself and earn twice what I am able to give him.  But, after all, if he is satisfied, why should I put ideas in his head?"

"Why, indeed? You seem most fortunate in having an employee who comes under the full market price.  It is not a common experience among employers in this age.  I don't know that your assistant is not as remarkable as your advertisement."

"Oh, he has his faults, too," said Mr. Wilson. "Never was such a fellow so obsessed with photography!  Snapping away with a camera when he ought to be improving his mind, and then diving down into the cellar like a rabbit into its hole to develop his film.  That is his main fault ... but on the whole he's a good worker.  There's no vice in him."

"He is still with you, I presume?"

"Yes, sir.  He and a girl of fourteen, who does a bit of simple cooking and keeps the place clean—that's all I have in the house, for I am a widower and never had any family.  We live very quietly, sir, the three of us; and we keep a roof over our heads and pay our debts, if we do nothing more.

"The first thing that put us out was that

advertisement.  Spaulding, he came down into the office just this day eight weeks ago, with this very paper in his hand, and he said:

"'I wish to the Lord, Mr. Wilson, that I was a red-headed man.'

"'Why is that?' I asked.

"'Why,' he said, 'here's another vacancy on the League of the Red-Headed Men.  It's worth quite a little fortune to any man who gets it, and I understand that there are more vacancies than there are men, so that the trustees are at their wits' end what to do with the money.  If my hair would only change color, here's a nice little crib all ready for me to step into.'

"'Why, what is it, then?' I asked.  You see, Mr. Holmes, I am a very stay-at-home man, and as my business came to me instead of my having to go to it, I was often weeks on end without putting my foot over the doormat.  In that way, I didn't know much of what was going on outside, and I was always glad of a bit of news.

"'Have you never heard of the League of the Red-Headed Men?' he asked with his eyes open.

"'Never.'

"'Why, I wonder at that, for you are eligible yourself for one of the vacancies!'

"'And what are they worth?' I asked.

"'Oh, merely a couple of hundred pounds per year, but the work is slight, and it need not interfere very much with one's other occupations.'

"Well, you can easily think that that made me prick up my ears, for the business has not been over-good for some years, and an extra couple of hundred pounds would have been very handy.

"'Tell me all about it,' I said.

"'Well,' he said, showing me the advertisement,

'you can see for yourself that the League has a vacancy, and there is the address where you should apply for particulars. As far as I can make out, the League was founded by an American millionaire—Ezekiah Hopkins—who was very peculiar in his ways. He was himself red-headed, and he had a great sympathy for all red-headed men; so when he died, it was found that he had left his enormous fortune in the hands of trustees, with instructions to apply the interest to the providing of easy berths to men whose hair is of that color. From all I hear, it is splendid pay and very little to do.'

"'But,' I said, 'there would be millions of red-headed men who would apply.'

"'Not so many as you might think,' he answered. 'You see, it is really confined to Londoners, and to grown men. This American had started from London when he was young, and he wanted to do the old town a good turn. Then again, I have heard it is no use your applying if your hair is light red, or dark red, or anything but real bright, blazing, fiery red. Now, if you cared to apply, Mr. Wilson, you would just walk in; but perhaps it would hardly be worth your while to put yourself out of the way for the sake of a few hundred pounds.'

"Now, it is a fact, gentlemen, as you may see for yourselves, that my hair is of a very full and rich tint, so that it seemed to me that if there was to be any competition in the matter, I stood as good a chance as any man that I had ever met. Vincent Spaulding seemed to know so much about it that I thought he might prove useful, so I just ordered him to put up the shutters for the day and to come right away with me. He was very willing to have a holiday, so we shut the business up and started off for the address that was given us in the advertisement.

"I never hope to see such a sight as that again, Mr. Holmes.  From north, south, east, and west ... every man who had a shade of red in his hair had tramped into the city to answer the advertisement! Fleet Street was choked with red-headed folk, and Pope's Court looked like a coster's orange barrow. I should not have thought there were so many in the whole country as were brought together by that single advertisement!     Every shade of color they were—straw, lemon, orange, brick, Irish-setter, liver, clay; but, as Spaulding said, there were not many who had the real, vivid, flame-colored tint.  When I saw how many were waiting, I would have given it up in despair; but Spaulding would not hear of it.  How he did it I could not imagine, but he pushed and pulled and butted until he got me through the crowd, and right up to the steps which led to the office. There was a double stream upon the stair, some going up in hope, and some coming back dejected; but we wedged in as well as we could and soon found ourselves in the office."

"Your experience has been a most entertaining one," remarked Holmes as his client paused. "Please, continue your very interesting statement."

"There was nothing in the office but a couple of wooden chairs and a deal table, behind which sat a small man with a head that was even redder than mine.  He said a few words to each candidate as he came up, and then he always managed to find some fault in them which would disqualify them.  Getting a vacancy did not seem to be such a very easy matter, after all. However, when our turn came the little man was much more favorable to me than to any of the others, and he closed the door as we entered, so that he might have a private word with us.

"'This is Mr. Jabez Wilson,' said my assistant, 'and he is willing to fill a vacancy in the League.'

"'And he is admirably suited for it,' the other answered. 'He has every requirement. I cannot recall when I have seen anything so fine.' He took a step backward, cocked his head on one side, and gazed at my hair until I felt quite bashful. Then suddenly he plunged forward, wrung my hand, and congratulated me warmly on my success.

"'It would be injustice to hesitate,' he said. 'You will, however, I am sure, excuse me for taking an obvious precaution.' With that, he seized my hair in both his hands, and tugged until I yelled with the pain! 'There are tears in your eyes,' he said as he released me. 'I perceive that all is as it should be. But we have to be careful, for we have twice been deceived by wigs and once by paint. I could tell you tales of cobbler's wax which would disgust you with human nature.' He stepped over to the window and shouted through it at the top of his voice that the vacancy was filled. A groan of disappointment came up from below, and the folk all trooped away in different directions until there was not a red-head to be seen except my own and that of the manager.

"'My name,' he said, 'is Mr. Duncan Ross, and I am myself one of the pensioners upon the fund left by our noble benefactor. Are you a married man, Mr. Wilson? Have you a family?'

"I answered that I had not.

"His face fell immediately.

"'Dear me!' he said gravely, 'that is very serious indeed! I am sorry to hear you say that. The fund was, of course, for the propagation and spread of the red-heads as well as for their maintenance. It is exceedingly unfortunate that you should be a bachelor.'

"My face lengthened at this, Mr. Holmes, for I thought that I was not to have the vacancy after all; but after thinking it over for a few minutes, he said that it would be all right.

"'In the case of another,' he said, 'the objection might be fatal, but we must stretch a point in favor of a man with such a head of hair as yours! When shall you be able to enter upon your new duties?'

"'Well, it is a little awkward, for I have a business already,' I said.

"'Oh, never mind about that, Mr. Wilson!' said Vincent Spaulding. 'I should be able to look after that for you.'

"'What would be the hours?' I asked.

"'Ten to two.'

"Now, a pawnbroker's business is mostly done of an evening, Mr. Holmes, especially Thursday and Friday evening, which is just before pay-day; so it would suit me very well to earn a little in the mornings. Besides, I knew that my assistant was a good man, and that he would see to anything that turned up.

"'That would suit me very well,' I said. 'And the pay?'

"'Is 4 pounds a week.'

"'And the work?'

"'Is purely nominal.'

"'What do you call "purely nominal"?'

"'Well, you have to be in the office, or at least in the building, the whole time. If you leave, you forfeit your whole position forever. The will is very clear upon that point. You don't comply with the conditions if you budge from the office during that time.'

"'It's only four hours a day, and I should not think of leaving,' I said.

"'No excuse will avail,' said Mr. Duncan Ross; 'neither sickness nor business nor anything else. There you must stay, or you lose your claim.'

"'And the work?'

"'Is to copy out the "Encyclopedia Britannica." There is the first volume of it in that press. You must find your own ink, pens, and blotting-paper, but we provide this table and chair. Will you be ready tomorrow?'

"'Certainly,' I answered.

"'Then, goodbye, Mr. Jabez Wilson, and let me congratulate you once more on the important position which you have been fortunate enough to gain.' He bowed me out of the room and I went home with my assistant, hardly knowing what to say or do, I was so pleased at my own good fortune.

"Well, I thought over the matter all day, and by evening I was in low spirits again; for I had quite persuaded myself that the whole affair must be some great hoax or fraud, though what its object might be I could not imagine. It seemed altogether past belief that anyone could make such a will, or that they would pay such a sum for doing anything so simple as copying out the 'Encyclopedia Britannica.' Vincent Spaulding did what he could to cheer me up, but by bedtime I had reasoned myself out of the whole thing. However, in the morning I determined to have a look at it anyhow, so I bought a penny bottle of ink, and with a quill-pen, and seven sheets of foolscap paper, I started off for Pope's Court.

"Well, to my surprise and delight, everything was as right as possible. The table was set out ready for me, and Mr. Duncan Ross was there to see that I got fairly to work.  He started me off upon the letter A, and then he left me; but he would drop in from time to time to see that all was right with me.  At two o'clock he bade me good-day, complimented me upon the amount that I had written, and locked the door of the office after me.

"This went on day after day, Mr. Holmes, and on Saturday the manager came in and planked down four golden sovereigns for my week's work.  It was the same next week, and the same the week after.  Every morning I was there at ten, and every afternoon I left at two.  By degrees, Mr. Duncan Ross took to coming in only once of a morning, and then, after a time, he did not come in at all.  Still, of course, I never dared to leave the room for an instant, for I was not sure when he might come, and the position was such a good one, and suited me so well, that I would not risk the loss of it.

"Eight weeks passed away like this, and I had written about Abbots and Archery and Armor and Architecture and Attica, and hoped with diligence that I might get on to the B's before very long.  It cost me something in paper, and I had pretty nearly filled a shelf with my writings.  And then, suddenly, the whole business came to an end!"

"To an end?"

"Yes, sir.  And no later than this morning.  I went to my work as usual at ten o'clock, but the door was shut and locked, with a little square of cardboard hammered on to the middle of the panel with a tack.  Here it is, and you can read for yourself."

He held up a piece of white cardboard about the size of a sheet of note-paper.  It read in this fashion:

## THE RED-HEADED LEAGUE
## IS
## DISSOLVED
## October 9, 1890

Sherlock Holmes and I surveyed this curt announcement and the rueful face behind it, until the comical side of the affair so completely overtopped every other consideration that we both burst out into a roar of laughter.

"I cannot see that there is anything very funny," cried our client, flushing up to the roots of his flaming head. "If you can do nothing better than laugh at me, I can go elsewhere."

"No, no," cried Holmes, shoving him back into the chair from which he had half risen. "I really wouldn't miss your case for the world. It is most refreshingly unusual. But there is, if you will excuse my saying so, something just a little funny about it. Please, what steps did you take when you found the card upon the door?"

"I was staggered, sir! I did not know what to do. Then I called at the offices round, but none of them seemed to know anything about it. Finally, I went to the landlord, who is an accountant living on the ground-floor, and I asked him if he could tell me what had become of the Red-headed League. He said that he had never heard of any such body! Then I asked him who Mr. Duncan Ross was. He answered that the name was new to him.

"'Well,' said I, 'the gentleman at No. 4.'

"'What, the red-headed man?'

"'Yes.'

"'Oh,' he said, 'his name was William Morris. He was a solicitor and was using my room as a temporary convenience until his new premises were ready.  He moved out yesterday.'

"'Where could I find him?'

"'Oh, at his new offices.  He did tell me the address ... Yes!  17 King Edward Street, near St. Paul's.'

"I started off, Mr. Holmes, but when I got to that address it was a manufactory of artificial knee-caps, and no one in it had ever heard of either Mr. William Morris or Mr. Duncan Ross."

"And what did you do then?" asked Holmes.

"I went home to Saxe-Coburg Square, and I took the advice of my assistant.  But he could not help me in any way.  He could only say that if I waited I should hear by post.  But that was not quite good enough, Mr. Holmes!  I did not wish to lose such a place without a struggle ... so, as I had heard that you were good enough to give advice to poor folk who were in need of it, I came right away to you."

"And you did very wisely," said Holmes.  "Your case is an exceedingly remarkable one, and I shall be happy to look into it.  From what you have told me, I think that it is possible that graver issues hang from it than might at first sight appear."

"Grave enough!" said Wilson.  "Why, I have lost four pound a week."

"As far as you are personally concerned," remarked Holmes, "I do not see that you have any grievance against this extraordinary league.  On the contrary, you are, as I understand, richer by some 30 pounds, to say nothing of the minute knowledge which you have gained on every subject which comes under the letter A.  You have lost nothing by them."

"No, sir.  But I want to find out about them, and

who they are, and what their object was in playing this prank—if it was a prank—upon me. It was a pretty expensive joke for them, for it cost them thirty-two pounds."

"We shall endeavor to clear up these points for you. And, first, one or two questions, Mr. Wilson: This assistant of yours who first called your attention to the advertisement—how long had he been with you?"

"About a month then."

"How did he come?"

"In answer to an advertisement."

"Was he the only applicant?"

"No, I had a dozen."

"Why did you pick him?"

"Because he was handy and would come cheap."

"At half-wages, in fact."

"Yes."

"What is he like, this Vincent Spaulding?"

"Small, stout-built, very quick in his ways, no hair on his face, though he's not short of thirty. Has a white splash of acid upon his forehead."

Holmes sat up in his chair in considerable excitement. "I thought as much," he said. "Have you ever observed that his ears are pierced for earrings?"

"Yes, sir. He told me that a gipsy had done it for him when he was a lad."

"Hmm!" Holmes said, sinking back in deep thought. "He is still with you?"

"Oh, yes, sir; I have only just left him."

"And has your business been attended to in your absence?"

"Nothing to complain of, sir. There's never very much to do of a morning."

"That will do, Mr. Wilson. I shall be happy to give

you an opinion upon the subject in the course of a day or two.  Today is Saturday, and I hope that by Monday we may come to a conclusion."

"Well, Watson," said Holmes when our visitor had left us, "what do you make of it all?"

"I make nothing of it," I answered frankly.  "It is a most mysterious business."

"As a rule," said Holmes, "the more bizarre a thing is the less mysterious it proves to be.  It is your commonplace, featureless crimes which are really puzzling, just as a commonplace face is the most difficult to identify.  But I must be prompt over this matter."

"What are you going to do, then?" I asked.

"To think," he answered.  He curled himself up in his chair, with his thin knees drawn up to his hawk-like nose, and there he sat with his eyes closed.  I had come to the conclusion that he had dropped asleep, and indeed was nodding myself, when he suddenly sprang out of his chair with the gesture of a man who has made up his mind.

"Sarasate plays at the St. James's Hall this afternoon," he remarked.  "What do you think, Watson? Could your patients spare you for a few hours?"

"I have nothing to do today.  My practice is never very absorbing."

"Then put on your hat and come!  I am going through the City first, and we can have some lunch on the way.  I observe that there is a good deal of German music on the program, which is rather more to my taste than Italian or French.  It is introspective, and I want to think.  Come along!"

We traveled by the Underground as far as Aldersgate; and a short walk took us to Saxe-Coburg

Square, the scene of the singular story which we had listened to in the morning.  It was a poky, little, shabby-genteel place, where four lines of dingy two-storied brick houses looked out into a small railed-in enclosure, where a lawn of weedy grass and a few clumps of faded laurel-bushes made a hard fight against a smoke-laden and uncongenial atmosphere.  Three gilt balls and a brown board with "JABEZ WILSON" in white letters, upon a corner house, announced the place where our red-headed client carried on his business. Sherlock Holmes stopped in front of it with his head on one side and looked it all over, with his eyes shining brightly between puckered lids.  Then he walked slowly up the street, and then down again to the corner, still looking keenly at the houses.  Finally he returned to the pawnbroker's, and, having thumped vigorously upon the pavement with his walking stick two or three times, he went up to the door and knocked. It was instantly opened by a bright-looking, clean-shaven young fellow, who asked him to step in.

"Thank you," said Holmes, "I only wished to ask you how you would go from here to the Strand."

"Third right, fourth left," answered the assistant promptly, closing the door.

"Smart fellow, that," observed Holmes as we walked away.  "He is, in my judgment, the fourth smartest man in London, and for daring I am not sure that he has not a claim to be third.  I have known something of him before."

"Evidently," I said, "Mr. Wilson's assistant counts for a good deal in this mystery of the Red-Headed League. I am sure that you inquired your way merely in order that you might see him."

"Not him."

"What then?"

"The knees of his trousers."

"And what did you see?"

"What I expected to see."

"Why did you beat the pavement?"

"My dear doctor, this is a time for observation, not for talk. We are spies in an enemy's country. We know something of Saxe-Coburg Square. Let us now explore the parts which lie behind it."

The road in which we found ourselves as we turned round the corner from the retired Saxe-Coburg Square presented as great a contrast to it as the front of a picture does to the back. It was one of the main arteries which conveyed the traffic of the City to the north and west. The roadway was blocked with the immense stream of commerce flowing in a double tide inward and outward, while the footpaths were black with the hurrying swarm of pedestrians. It was difficult to realize as we looked at the line of fine shops and stately business premises that they really abutted on the other side upon the faded and stagnant square which we had just quitted.

"Let me see," said Holmes, standing at the corner and glancing along the line, "I should like just to remember the order of the houses here. It is a hobby of mine to have an exact knowledge of London. There is Mortimer's, the tobacconist, the little newspaper shop, the Coburg branch of the City and Suburban Bank, the Vegetarian Restaurant, and McFarlane's carriage-building depot. That carries us right on to the other block. And now, Doctor, we've done our work, so it's time we had some play. A sandwich and a cup of coffee, and then off to violin-land, where all is sweetness and delicacy and harmony, and there are no red-headed clients to vex us with their mysteries."

My friend was an enthusiastic musician, being himself not only a very capable performer but a composer of no ordinary merit. All the afternoon he sat in the stalls, wrapped in the most perfect happiness, gently waving his long, thin fingers in time to the music, while his gently smiling face and his languid, dreamy eyes were as unlike those of Holmes the sleuth-hound, Holmes the relentless, keen-witted, ready-handed criminal agent, as it was possible to conceive. In his singular character the dual nature alternately asserted itself, and his extreme exactness and astuteness represented, as I have often thought, the reaction against the poetic and contemplative mood which occasionally predominated him. The swing of his nature took him from extreme languor to devouring energy; and, as I knew well, he was never so truly formidable as when, for days on end, he had been lounging in his armchair amid his improvisations and his black-letter editions. Then it was that the lust of the chase would suddenly come upon him, and that his brilliant reasoning power would rise to the level of intuition—until those who were unacquainted with his methods would look askance at him as on a man whose knowledge was not that of other mortals! When I saw him that afternoon, so enwrapped in the music at St. James's Hall, I felt that an evil time might be coming upon those whom he had set himself to hunt down.

"You want to go home, no doubt, Doctor," he remarked as we emerged.

"Yes, it would be as well."

"And I have some business to do which will take some hours. This business at Coburg Square is serious."

"Why serious?"

"A considerable crime is in contemplation. I have every reason to believe that we shall be in time to stop it. But today being Saturday rather complicates matters. I shall want your help tonight."

"At what time?"

"Ten will be early enough."

"I shall be at Baker Street at ten."

"Very well. And, I say, Doctor, there may be some little danger, so kindly put your army revolver in your pocket." He waved his hand, turned on his heel, and disappeared in an instant among the crowd.

I trust that I am not more dense than my neighbors, but I was always oppressed with a sense of my own stupidity in my dealings with Sherlock Holmes. Here I had heard what he had heard, I had seen what he had seen ... and yet from his words it was evident that he saw clearly not only what had happened but what was about to happen, while to me the whole business was still confused and grotesque. As I drove home to my house in Kensington I thought over it all, from the extraordinary story of the red-headed copier of the "Encyclopedia" down to the visit to Saxe-Coburg Square, and the ominous words with which he had parted from me.

What was this nocturnal expedition, and why should I go armed? Where were we going, and what were we to do? I had the hint from Holmes that this smooth-faced pawnbroker's assistant was a formidable man—a man who might play a deep game. I tried to puzzle it out, but gave it up in despair and set the matter aside until night should bring an explanation.

It was a quarter-past nine when I started from home and made my way across the Park, and so through Oxford Street to Baker Street. Two carriages were standing at the door, and as I entered the passage, I heard the sound of voices from above. On entering his room, I found Holmes in animated conversation with two men, one of whom I recognized as Peter Jones, the official police agent, while the other was a long, thin, sad-faced man, with a very shiny hat and oppressively respectable frock-coat.

"Ha! Our party is complete," said Holmes, buttoning up his pea-jacket and taking his heavy hunting crop from the rack. "Watson, I think you know Mr. Jones, of Scotland Yard? Let me introduce you to Mr. Merryweather, who is to be our companion in tonight's adventure."

"We're hunting in couples again, Doctor, you see," said Jones in his consequential way. "Our friend here is a wonderful man for starting a chase. All he wants is an old dog to help him to do the running down."

"I hope a wild goose may not prove to be at the end of our chase!" observed Mr. Merryweather gloomily.

"You may place considerable confidence in Mr. Holmes, sir," said the police agent loftily. "He has his own little methods, which are, if he won't mind my saying so, just a little too theoretical and fantastic, but he has the makings of a detective in him. It is not too much to say that once or twice, he has been more nearly correct than the official force."

"Oh, if you say so, Mr. Jones," said the stranger with deference.

"I think you will find," said Sherlock Holmes, "that you will play for a higher stake tonight than you have ever done yet, and that the play will be more exciting.

For you, Mr. Merryweather, the stake will be some 30,000 pounds; and for you, Jones, it will be the man upon whom you wish to lay your hands."

"John Clay—the murderer, thief, smasher, and forger! He's a young man, Mr. Merryweather, but he is at the head of his profession, and I would rather have my handcuffs on him than on any criminal in London. He's a remarkable man, young John Clay. His grandfather was a royal duke, and he himself has been to Eton and Oxford. His brain is as cunning as his fingers, and though we find signs of him at every turn, we never know where to find the man himself! I've been on his track for years and have never set eyes on him yet."

"I hope that I may have the pleasure of introducing you tonight. I've had one or two little turns also with Mr. John Clay, and I agree with you that he is at the head of his profession. It is past ten, however, and quite time that we started. If you two will take the first carriage, Watson and I will follow in the second."

Sherlock Holmes was not very communicative during the long drive and lay back in the cab humming the tunes which he had heard in the afternoon. We rattled through an endless labyrinth of gas-lit streets until we emerged into Farrington Street.

"We are close now," my friend remarked. "This fellow Merryweather is a bank director, and personally interested in the matter. I thought it as well to have Jones with us also. He is not a bad fellow, though an absolute imbecile in his profession. He has one positive virtue. He is as brave as a bulldog and as tenacious as a lobster if he gets his claws upon anyone. Here we are, and they are waiting for us."

We had reached the same crowded thoroughfare in which we had found ourselves in the morning. Our cabs were dismissed, and, following the guidance of Mr. Merryweather, we passed down a narrow passage and through a side door, which he opened for us. Within there was a small corridor, which ended in a very massive iron gate. This also was opened, and led down a flight of winding stone steps, which terminated at another formidable gate. Mr. Merryweather stopped to light a lantern, and then conducted us down a dark, earth-smelling passage, and so, after opening a third door, into a huge vault or cellar, which was piled all round with crates and massive boxes.

"You are not very vulnerable from above," Holmes remarked as he held up the lantern and gazed about him.

"Nor from below," said Mr. Merryweather, striking his walking stick upon the flags which lined the floor. "Why, dear me, it sounds quite hollow!" he remarked, looking up in surprise.

"I must really ask you to be a little more quiet!" said Holmes severely. "You have already imperilled the whole success of our expedition. Might I beg that you would have the goodness to sit down upon one of those boxes, and not to interfere?"

The solemn Mr. Merryweather perched himself upon a crate, with a very injured expression upon his face, while Holmes fell upon his knees upon the floor and, with the lantern and a magnifying lens, began to examine minutely the cracks between the stones. A few seconds sufficed to satisfy him, for he sprang to his feet again and put his glass in his pocket.

"We have at least an hour before us," he

remarked quietly, "for they can hardly take any steps until the good pawnbroker is safely in bed. Then they will not lose a minute, for the sooner they do their work the longer time they will have for their escape. We are at present, Doctor—as no doubt you have divined—in the cellar of the City branch of one of the principal London banks.  Mr. Merryweather is the chairman of directors, and he will explain to you that there are reasons why the more daring criminals of London should take a considerable interest in this cellar at present."

"It is our French gold," whispered the director. "We have had several warnings that an attempt might be made upon it."

"Your French gold?"

"Yes.  We had occasion some months ago to strengthen our resources and borrowed for that purpose 30,000 napoleons from the Bank of France. It has become known that we have never had occasion to unpack the money, and that it is still lying in our cellar.  The crate upon which I sit contains 2,000 napoleons packed between layers of lead foil. Our reserve of bullion is much larger at present than is usually kept in a single branch office, and the directors have had misgivings upon the subject."

"Which were very well justified," observed Holmes.  "And now it is time that we arranged our little plans.  I expect that within an hour matters will come to a head.  In the meantime, Mr. Merryweather, we must put the screen over that dark lantern."

"And sit in the dark?"

"I am afraid so. The enemy's preparations have gone so far that we cannot risk the presence of a light. And, first of all, we must choose our positions. These are daring men, and though we shall take them at a disadvantage, they may do us some harm unless we are careful. I shall stand behind this crate, and do you conceal yourselves behind those. Then, when I flash a light upon them, close in swiftly. If they fire, Watson, have no compunction about shooting them down."

I placed my revolver, cocked, upon the top of the wooden case behind which I crouched. Holmes shot the slide across the front of his lantern and left us in pitch darkness—such an absolute darkness as I have never before experienced. The smell of hot metal remained to assure us that the light was still there, ready to flash out at a moment's notice. To me, with my nerves worked up to a pitch of expectancy, there was something depressing and subduing in the sudden gloom, and in the cold dank air of the vault.

"They have but one retreat," whispered Holmes. "That is back through the house into Saxe-Coburg Square. I hope that you have done what I asked you, Jones?"

"I have an inspector and two officers waiting at the front door."

"Then we have stopped all the holes. And now we must be silent and wait."

What a time it seemed! From comparing notes afterwards it was but an hour and a quarter, yet it appeared to me that the night must have almost gone and the dawn be breaking above us. My limbs were weary and stiff, for I feared to change my position; yet my nerves were worked up to the highest pitch of tension, and my hearing was so acute that I could not only hear the gentle breathing of my companions, but I could distinguish the deeper, heavier breathing of the bulky Jones from the thin, sighing note of the bank director.  From my position I could look over the case in the direction of the floor.

Suddenly, my eyes caught the glint of a light!

At first it was but a lurid spark upon the stone pavement.  Then it lengthened out until it became a yellow line, and then, without any warning or sound, a gash seemed to open and a hand appeared, a white, almost womanly hand, which felt about in the center of the little area of light.  For a minute or more the hand, with its writhing fingers, protruded out of the floor.  Then it was withdrawn as suddenly as it appeared, and all was dark again save the single lurid spark which marked a chink between the stones.

Its disappearance, however, was but momentary.  With a rending, tearing sound, one of the broad, white stones turned over upon its side and left a square, gaping hole, through which streamed the light of a lantern.  Over the edge there peeped a clean-cut, boyish face, which looked keenly about it, and then, with a hand on either side of the aperture, drew itself shoulder-high and waist-high, until one knee rested upon the edge.  In another instant he stood at the side of the hole and was hauling after him a companion, lithe and small like himself, with a pale face and a shock of very red hair.

"It's all clear," he whispered.  "Have you the chisel and the bags?  Great Scott!  Jump, Archie, jump, and I'll swing for it!"

Sherlock Holmes had sprung out and seized the intruder by the collar.  The other dived down the hole, and I heard the sound of rending cloth as Jones clutched at him.  The light flashed upon the barrel of a revolver, but Holmes' hunting crop came down on the man's wrist, and the pistol clinked upon the stone floor.

"It's no use, John Clay," said Holmes blandly. "You have no chance at all."

"So I see," the other answered with the utmost coolness. "I fancy that my pal is all right, though I see you have got his coattails."

"There are three men waiting for him at the door," said Holmes.

"Oh, indeed! You seem to have done the thing very completely. I must compliment you."

"And I you," Holmes answered. "Your red-headed idea was very new and effective."

"You'll see your pal again presently," said Jones. "He's quicker at climbing down holes than I am. Just hold out while I fix the derbies."

"I beg that you will not touch me with your filthy hands," remarked our prisoner as the handcuffs clattered upon his wrists. "You may not be aware that I have royal blood in my veins. Have the goodness, also, when you address me always to say 'sir' and 'please.'"

"All right," said Jones with a stare and a snigger. "Well, would you please, sir, march upstairs, where we can get a cab to carry your Highness to the police-station?"

"That is better," said John Clay serenely. He made a sweeping bow to the three of us and walked quietly off in the custody of the detective.

"Really, Mr. Holmes," said Mr. Merryweather as we followed them from the cellar, "I do not know how the bank can thank you or repay you. There is no doubt that you have detected and defeated in the most complete manner one of the most determined attempts at bank robbery that have ever come within my experience."

"I have had one or two little scores of my own to settle with Mr. John Clay," said Holmes. "I have been at some small expense over this matter, which I shall expect the bank to refund, but beyond that I am amply repaid by having had an experience which is in many ways unique, and by hearing the very remarkable narrative of the Red-Headed League."

"You see, Watson," he explained in the early hours of the morning as we sat over a glass of whisky and soda in Baker Street, "it was perfectly obvious from the first that the only possible object of this rather fantastic business of the advertisement of the League, and the copying of the 'Encyclopedia,' must be to get this not over-bright pawnbroker out of the way for a number of hours every day. It was a curious way of managing it, but, really, it would be difficult to suggest a better. The method was no doubt suggested to Clay's ingenious mind by the color of his accomplice's hair. The 4 pounds a week was a lure which must draw him, and what was it to them, who were playing for thousands? They put in the advertisement, one rogue has the temporary office, the other rogue incites the man to apply for it, and together they manage to secure his absence every morning in the week. From the time that I heard of the assistant having come for half wages, it was obvious to me that he had some strong motive for securing the situation."

"But how could you guess what the motive was?"

"Had there been women in the house, I should have suspected a more *vulgar* intrigue. That, however, was out of the question. The man's business was a small one, and there was nothing in his house which could account for such elaborate preparations, and such an expenditure as they were at. It must, then, be something out of the house. What could it be? I thought of the assistant's fondness for photography, and his trick of vanishing into the cellar. The cellar! There was the end of this tangled clue. Then I made inquiries as to this mysterious assistant and found that I had to deal with one of the coolest and most daring criminals in London. He was doing something in the cellar—something which took many hours a day for months on end. What could it be, once more? I could think of nothing save that he was running a tunnel to some other building.

"So far I had got when we went to visit the scene of action. I surprised you by beating upon the pavement with my stick. I was ascertaining whether the cellar stretched out in front or behind. It was not in front. Then I rang the bell, and, as I hoped, the assistant answered it. We have had some skirmishes, but we had never set eyes upon each other before. I hardly looked at his face. His knees were what I wished to see. You must yourself have remarked how worn, wrinkled, and stained they were. They spoke of those hours of burrowing. The only remaining point was what they were burrowing for. I walked round the corner, saw the City and Suburban Bank abutted on our friend's premises, and felt that I had solved my problem. When you drove home after the concert I called upon Scotland Yard and upon the chairman of the bank directors, with the result that you have seen."

"And how could you tell that they would make their attempt tonight?" I asked.

"Well, when they closed their League offices, that was a sign that they cared no longer about Mr. Jabez Wilson's presence—in other words, that they had completed their tunnel.  But it was essential that they should use it soon, as it might be discovered, or the bullion might be removed.  Saturday would suit them better than any other day, as it would give them two days for their escape.  For all these reasons, I expected them to come tonight."

"You reasoned it out beautifully," I exclaimed in unfeigned admiration.  "It is so long a chain, and yet every link rings true."

"It saved me from boredom," he answered, yawning.  "Alas!  I already feel it closing in upon me again.  My life is spent in one long effort to escape from the commonplaces of existence.  These little problems help me to do so."

"And you are a benefactor of the race," I said.

He shrugged his shoulders.  "Well, perhaps, after all, it is of some little use," he remarked.  "'L'homme c'est rien—l'oeuvre c'est tout,' as Gustave Flaubert wrote to George Sand."

# 3<sup>rd</sup> ADVENTURE!
# A CASE OF IDENTITY

"My dear fellow," said Sherlock Holmes as we sat on either side of the fire in his lodgings at Baker Street, "life is infinitely stranger than anything which the mind of man could invent. We would not dare to conceive the things which are really mere commonplaces of existence. If we could fly out of that window hand in hand, hover over this great city, gently remove the roofs, and peep in at the queer things which are going on, the strange coincidences, the plannings, the cross-purposes, the wonderful chains of events, working through generations, and leading to the most excessive results, it would make all fiction with its conventionalities and foreseen conclusions most stale and unprofitable."

"And yet I am not convinced of it," I answered. "The cases which come to light in the papers are, as a rule, bald enough, and vulgar enough. We have in our police reports realism pushed to its extreme limits, and yet the result is, it must be confessed, neither fascinating nor artistic."

"A certain selection and discretion must be used in producing a realistic effect," remarked Holmes. "This is wanting in the police report, where more stress is laid, perhaps, upon the platitudes of the magistrate than upon the details, which to an observer contain the vital essence of the whole matter. Depend upon it, there is nothing so unnatural as the commonplace."

I smiled and shook my head. "I can quite understand your thinking so," I said. "Of course, in your position of unofficial adviser and helper to everybody who is absolutely puzzled, throughout three continents, you are brought in contact with all that is strange and bizarre. But here"—I picked up the morning paper from the ground—"let us put it to a practical test. Here is the first heading upon which I come. 'A husband's cruelty to his wife.' There is half a column of print, but I know without reading it that it is all perfectly familiar to me. There is, of course, the other woman, the drink, the push, the blow, the bruise, the sympathetic sister or landlady. The crudest of writers could invent nothing more crude."

"Indeed, your example is an unfortunate one for your argument," said Holmes, taking the paper and glancing his eye down it. "This is the Dundas separation case, and, as it happens, I was engaged in clearing up some small points in connection with it. The husband was a teetotaler, there was no other woman, and the conduct complained of was that he had drifted into the habit of winding up every meal by taking out his false teeth and hurling them at his wife, which, you will allow, is not an action likely to occur to the imagination of the average story-teller. Take a pinch of snuff, Doctor, and acknowledge that I have scored over you in your example."

He held out his snuffbox of old gold, with a great amethyst in the center of the lid. Its splendor was in such contrast to his homely ways and simple life that I could not help commenting upon it.

"Ah," he said, "I forgot that I had not seen you for

some weeks. It is a little souvenir from the King of Bohemia in return for my assistance in the case of the Irene Adler papers."

"And the ring?" I asked, glancing at a remarkable brilliant which sparkled upon his finger.

"It was from the reigning family of Holland, though the matter in which I served them was of such delicacy that I cannot confide it even to you, who have been good enough to chronicle one or two of my little problems."

"And have you any on hand just now?" I asked with interest.

"Some ten or twelve, but none which present any feature of interest. They are important, you understand, without being interesting. Indeed, I have found that it is usually in unimportant matters that there is a field for the observation, and for the quick analysis of cause and effect which gives the charm to an investigation. The larger crimes are apt to be the simpler, for the bigger the crime the more obvious, as a rule, is the motive. In these cases, save for one rather intricate matter which has been referred to me from Marseilles, there is nothing which presents any features of interest. It is possible, however, that I may have something better before very many minutes are over, for this is one of my clients, or I am much mistaken."

He had risen from his chair and was standing between the parted blinds gazing down into the dull neutral-tinted London street. Looking over his shoulder, I saw that on the pavement opposite there stood a large woman with a heavy fur boa round her neck, and a large curling red feather in a broad-brimmed hat which was tilted in a flirtatious Duchess of Devonshire fashion over her ear. From under this great panoply she peeped up in a nervous, hesitating fashion at our windows, while her body oscillated backward and forward, and her fingers fidgeted with her glove buttons. Suddenly, with a plunge, as of the swimmer who leaves the bank, she hurried across the road, and we heard the sharp clang of the bell.

"I have seen those symptoms before," said Holmes. "Oscillation upon the pavement always means a love affair. She would like advice, but is not sure that the matter is not too delicate for communication. And yet even here we may discriminate. When a woman has been seriously wronged by a man she no longer oscillates, and the usual symptom is a broken bell wire. Here we may take it that there is a love matter, but that the maiden is not so much angry as perplexed, or grieved. But here she comes in person to resolve our doubts."

As he spoke there was a tap at the door, and the boy in buttons entered to announce Miss Mary Sutherland, while the lady herself loomed behind his small black figure like a full-sailed merchant-man behind a tiny pilot boat. Sherlock Holmes welcomed her with the easy courtesy for which he was remarkable, and, having closed the door and bowed her into an armchair, he looked her over in the minute and yet abstracted fashion which was peculiar to him.

"Do you not find," he said, "that with your short-sight it is a little trying to do so much typewriting?"

"I did at first," she answered, "but now I know where the letters are without looking." Then, suddenly realizing the full purport of his words, she gave a violent start and looked up, with fear and astonishment upon her broad, good-humored face. "You've heard about me, Mr. Holmes!" she cried.

"How else could you know that?"

"Never mind," said Holmes, laughing, "it is my business to know things. Perhaps I have trained myself to see what others overlook. If not, why should you come to consult me?"

"I came to you, sir, because I heard of you from Mrs. Etherege, whose husband you found so easy when the police and everyone had given him up for dead. Oh, Mr. Holmes, I wish you would do as much for me. I'm not rich, but still I have a hundred a year in my own right, besides the little that I make by the machine, and I would give it all to know what has become of Mr. Hosmer Angel."

"Why did you come away to consult me in such a hurry?" asked Sherlock Holmes, with his finger-tips together and his eyes to the ceiling.

Again a startled look came over the somewhat empty face of Miss Mary Sutherland. "Yes, I did bang out of the house," she said, "for it made me angry to see the easy way in which Mr. Windibank—that is, my father—took it all. He would not go to the police, and he would not go to you, and so at last, as he would do nothing and kept on saying that there was no harm done, it made me mad, and I just threw on my things and came right away to you."

"Your father," said Holmes, "your *step*father, surely, since the name is different."

"Yes, my stepfather. I call him father, though it sounds funny, too, for he is only five years and two months older than myself."

"And your mother is alive?"

"Oh, yes, mother is alive and well. I wasn't best pleased, Mr. Holmes, when she married again so soon after father's death, and a man who was nearly fifteen years younger than herself. Father was a plumber in the Tottenham Court Road, and he left a tidy business behind him, which mother carried on with Mr. Hardy, the foreman; but when Mr. Windibank came, he made her sell the business, for he was very superior, being a traveler in wines.  They got 4,700 pounds for the goodwill and interest, which wasn't near as much as father could have got if he had been alive."

I had expected to see Sherlock Holmes impatient under this rambling and inconsequential narrative, but, on the contrary, he had listened with the greatest concentration of attention.

"Your own little income," he asked, "does it come out of the business?"

"Oh, no, sir.  It is quite separate and was left me by my uncle Ned in Auckland.  It is in New Zealand stock, paying 4-½ percent.  Two-thousand-five-hundred pounds was the amount, but I can only touch the interest."

"You interest me extremely," said Holmes. "And since you draw so large a sum as a hundred a year, with what you earn into the bargain, you no doubt travel a little and indulge yourself in every way.  I believe that a single lady can get on very nicely upon an income of about 60 pounds."

"I could do with much less than that, Mr. Holmes, but you understand that as long as I live at home I don't wish to be a burden to them, and so they have the use of the money just while I am staying with them.  Of course, that is only just for the time.  Mr. Windibank draws my interest every quarter and pays it over to mother, and I find that I can do pretty well with what I earn at typewriting. It brings me twopence a sheet, and I can often do from fifteen to twenty sheets in a day."

"You have made your position very clear to me," said Holmes. "This is my friend, Dr. Watson, before whom you can speak as freely as before myself. Kindly tell us now all about your connection with Mr. Hosmer Angel."

A flush stole over Miss Sutherland's face, and she picked nervously at the fringe of her jacket. "I met him first at the gasfitters' ball," she said. "They used to send father tickets when he was alive, and then afterwards they remembered us, and sent them to mother. Mr. Windibank did not wish us to go. He never did wish us to go anywhere. He would get quite mad if I wanted so much as to join a Sunday-school treat. But this time I was set on going, and I would go; for what right had he to prevent? He said the folk were not fit for us to know, when all father's friends were to be there. And he said that I had nothing fit to wear, when I had my purple plush that I had never so much as taken out of the drawer. At last, when nothing else would do, he went off to France upon the business of the firm, but we went, mother and I, with Mr. Hardy, who used to be our foreman, and it was there I met Mr. Hosmer Angel."

"I suppose," said Holmes, "that when Mr. Windibank came back from France he was very annoyed at your having gone to the ball."

"Oh, well, he was very good about it. He laughed, I remember, and shrugged his shoulders, and said there was no use denying anything to a woman, for she would have her way."

"I see. Then at the gasfitters' ball you met, as I understand, a gentleman called Mr. Hosmer Angel."

"Yes, sir. I met him that night, and he called next day to ask if we had got home all safe, and after that we met him—that is to say, Mr. Holmes, I met him *twice* for walks, but after that father came back again, and Mr. Hosmer Angel could not come to the house anymore."

"No?"

"Well, you know father didn't like anything of the sort. He wouldn't have any visitors if he could help it, and he used to say that a woman should be happy in her own family circle. But then, as I used to say to mother, a woman wants her own circle to begin with, and I had not got mine yet."

"But how about Mr. Hosmer Angel? Did he make no attempt to see you?"

"Well, father was going off to France again in a week, and Hosmer wrote and said that it would be safer and better not to see each other until he had gone. We could write in the meantime, and he used to write every day. I took the letters in the morning, so there was no need for father to know."

"Were you engaged to the gentleman at this time?"

"Oh, yes, Mr. Holmes. We were engaged after the first walk that we took. Hosmer—Mr. Angel—was a cashier in an office in Leadenhall Street—and—"

"What office?"

"That's the worst of it, Mr. Holmes, I don't know."

"Where did he live, then?"

"He slept on the premises."

"And you don't know his address?"

"No—except that it was Leadenhall Street."

"Where did you address your letters, then?"

"To the Leadenhall Street Post Office, to be left till called for. He said that if they were sent to the office he would be teased by all the other clerks about having letters from a lady, so I offered to typewrite them, like he did his, but he wouldn't have that, for he said that when I wrote them they seemed to come from me, but when they were typewritten he always felt that the machine had come between us. That will just show you how fond he was of me, Mr. Holmes, and the little things that he would think of."

"It was most suggestive," said Holmes. "It has long been an axiom of mine that the little things are infinitely the most important. Can you remember any other little things about Mr. Hosmer Angel?"

"He was a very shy man, Mr. Holmes. He would rather walk with me in the evening than in the daylight, for he said that he hated to be conspicuous. Very retiring and gentlemanly he was. Even his voice was gentle. He'd had the quinsy and swollen glands when he was young, he told me, and it had left him with a weak throat, and a hesitating, whispering fashion of speech. He was always well dressed, very neat and plain, but his eyes were weak, just as mine are, and he wore tinted glasses against the glare."

"Well, and what happened when Mr. Windibank, your stepfather, returned to France?"

"Mr. Hosmer Angel came to the house again and proposed that we should marry before father came back. He was in dreadful earnest and made me swear, with my hands on the Testament, that whatever happened I would always be true to him. Mother said he was quite right to make me swear, and that it was a sign of his passion. Mother was all in his favor from the first and was even fonder of him than I was. Then, when they talked of marrying within the week, I began to ask about father; but they both said never to mind about father, but just to tell him afterwards, and mother said she would make it all right with him. I didn't quite like that, Mr. Holmes. It seemed funny that I should ask his leave, as he was only a few years older than me; but I didn't want to do anything on the sly, so I wrote to father at Bordeaux, where the company has its French offices, but the letter came back to me on the very morning of the wedding."

"It missed him, then?"

"Yes, sir; for he had started to England just before it arrived."

"Ha! That was unfortunate. Your wedding was arranged, then, for the Friday. Was it to be in church?"

"Yes, sir, but very quietly. It was to be at St. Saviour's, near King's Cross, and we were to have breakfast afterwards at the St. Pancras Hotel. Hosmer came for us in a carriage, but as there were two of us he put us both into it and stepped himself into a four-wheeler, which happened to be the only other cab in the street. We got to the church first, and when the four-wheeler drove up we waited for him to step out, but he never did, and when the cabman got down from the box and looked there was no one there! The cabman said that he could not imagine what had become of him, for he had seen him get in with his own eyes. That was last Friday, Mr. Holmes, and I have never seen or heard anything since then to throw any light upon what became of him."

"It seems to me that you have been very shamefully treated," said Holmes.

"Oh, no, sir! He was too good and kind to leave me so. Why, all the morning he was saying to me that, whatever happened, I was to be true; and that even if something quite unforeseen occurred to separate us, I was always to remember that I was pledged to him, and that he would claim his pledge sooner or later.  It seemed strange talk for a wedding-morning, but what has happened since gives a meaning to it."

"Most certainly it does.  Your own opinion is, then, that some unforeseen catastrophe has occurred to him?"

"Yes, sir.  I believe that he foresaw some danger, or else he would not have talked so.  And then I think that what he foresaw happened."

"But you have no notion as to what it could have been?"

"None."

"One more question.  How did your mother take the matter?"

"She was angry, and said that I was never to speak of the matter again."

"And your father? Did you tell him?"

"Yes; and he seemed to think, with me, that something had happened, and that I should hear of Hosmer again.  As he said, what interest could anyone have in bringing me to the doors of the church, and then leaving me?  Now, if he had borrowed my money, or if he had married me and got my money settled on him, there might be some reason, but Hosmer was very independent about money and never would look at a shilling of mine. And yet, what could have happened? And why could he not write?  Oh, it drives me half-mad to think of it, and I can't sleep a wink at night." She pulled a little handkerchief out of her muff and began to sob heavily into it.

"I shall glance into the case for you," said Holmes, rising, "and I have no doubt that we shall reach some definite result.  Let the weight of the matter rest upon me now, and do not let your mind dwell upon it further. Above all, try to let Mr. Hosmer Angel vanish from your memory, as he has done from your life."

"Then you don't think I'll see him again?"

"I fear not."

"Then what has happened to him?"

"You will leave that question in my hands. I should like an accurate description of him and any letters of his which you can spare."

"I advertised for him in last Saturday's Chronicle," she said. "Here is the slip and here are four letters from him."

"Thank you. And your address?"

"No. 31 Lyon Place, Camberwell."

"Mr. Angel's address you never had, I understand. Where is your father's place of business?"

"He travels for Westhouse & Marbank, the great claret importers of Fenchurch Street."

"Thank you. You have made your statement very clearly. You will leave the papers here, and remember the advice which I have given you. Let the whole incident be a sealed book, and do not allow it to affect your life."

"You are very kind, Mr. Holmes, but I cannot do that. I shall be true to Hosmer. He shall find me ready when he comes back."

For all the preposterous hat and the vacuous face, there was something noble in the simple faith of our visitor which compelled our respect. She laid her little bundle of papers upon the table and went her way, with a promise to come again whenever she might be summoned.

Sherlock Holmes sat silent for a few minutes with his fingertips still pressed together, his legs stretched out in front of him, and his gaze directed upward to the ceiling.

"Quite an interesting study, that maiden," he observed. "I found her more interesting than her little problem, which, by the way, is rather a trite one. You will find parallel cases, if you consult my index, in Andover in '77, and there was something of the sort at The Hague last year. Old as is the idea, however, there were one or two details which were new to me. But the maiden herself was most instructive."

"You appeared to read a good deal upon her which was quite invisible to me," I remarked.

"Not invisible but unnoticed, Watson. You did not know where to look, and so you missed all that was important.  I can never bring you to realize the importance of sleeves, the suggestiveness of thumbnails, or the great issues that may hang from a bootlace.  Now, what did you gather from that woman's appearance?  Describe it."

"Well, she had a slate-colored, broad-brimmed straw hat, with a feather of a brickish red. Her jacket was black, with black beads sewn upon it, and a fringe of little black jet ornaments. Her dress was brown, rather darker than coffee color, with a little purple plush at the neck and sleeves. Her gloves were greyish and were worn through at the right forefinger. Her boots I didn't observe. She had small round, hanging gold earrings, and a general air of being fairly well-to-do in a vulgar, comfortable, easy-going way."

Sherlock Holmes clapped his hands softly together and chuckled.

"Upon my word, Watson, you are coming along wonderfully. You have really done very well indeed. It is true that you have missed everything of importance, but you have hit upon the method, and you have a quick eye for color. Never trust to general impressions, my boy, but concentrate yourself upon details. My first glance is always at a woman's sleeve. In a man, it is perhaps better first to take the knee of the trouser. As you observe, this woman had plush upon her sleeves, which is a most useful material for showing traces. The double line a little above the wrist, where the typewritist presses against the table, was beautifully defined. The sewing-machine, of the hand type, leaves a similar mark, but only on the left arm, and on the side of it farthest from the thumb, instead of being right across the broadest part, as this was. I then glanced at her face, and, observing the dent of spectacles at either side of her nose, I ventured a remark upon short sight and typewriting, which seemed to surprise her."

"It surprised me."

"But, surely, it was obvious. I was then much surprised and interested on glancing down to observe that, though the boots which she was wearing were not mismatched, they were really odd ones; the one having a slightly decorated toe-cap, and the other a plain one. One was buttoned only in the two lower buttons out of five, and the other at the first, third, and fifth. Now, when you see that a young lady, otherwise neatly dressed, has come away from home with odd boots, half-buttoned, it is no great deduction to say that she came away in a hurry."

"And what else?" I asked, keenly interested, as I always was, by my friend's incisive reasoning.

"I noted, in passing, that she had written a note before leaving home but after being fully dressed. You observed that her right glove was torn at the forefinger, but you did not apparently see that both glove and finger were stained with violet ink. She had written in a hurry and dipped her pen too deep. It must have been this morning, or the mark would not remain clear upon the finger. All this is amusing, though rather elementary, but I must go back to business, Watson. Would you mind reading me the advertised description of Mr. Hosmer Angel?"

I held the little printed slip to the light.

"Missing," it said, "on the morning of the fourteenth, a gentleman named Hosmer Angel. About five ft., seven in. in height; strongly built, sallow complexion, black hair, a little bald in the center, bushy, black side-whiskers and moustache; tinted glasses, slight infirmity of speech. Was dressed, when last seen, in black frock-coat faced with silk, black waistcoat, gold Albert chain, and grey Harris tweed trousers, with brown gaiters over elastic-sided boots. Known to have been employed in an office in Leadenhall Street. Anybody bringing—"

"That will do," said Holmes. "As to the letters," he continued, glancing over them, "they are very commonplace. Absolutely no clue in them to Mr. Angel, save that he quotes Balzac once. There is one remarkable point, however, which will no doubt strike you."

"They are typewritten," I remarked.

"Not only that, but the signature is typewritten. Look at the neat little 'Hosmer Angel' at the bottom. There is a date, you see, but no superscription except Leadenhall Street, which is rather vague. The point about the signature is very suggestive —in fact, we may call it conclusive."

"Of what?"

"My dear fellow, is it possible you do not see how strongly it bears upon the case?"

"I cannot say that I do, unless it were that he wished to be able to deny his signature if an action for breach of promise were instituted."

"No, that was not the point. However, I shall write two letters, which should settle the matter. One is to a firm in the City, the other is to the young lady's stepfather, Mr. Windibank, asking him whether he could meet us here at six o'clock tomorrow evening. It is just as well that we should do business with the male relatives. And now, Doctor, we can do nothing until the answers to those letters come, so we may put our little problem upon the shelf for the interim."

I had had so many reasons to believe in my friend's subtle powers of reasoning and extraordinary energy in action that I felt that he must have some solid grounds for the assured and easy demeanor with which he treated the singular mystery which he had been called upon to fathom. Once only had I known him to fail, in the case of the King of Bohemia and of the Irene Adler photograph; but when I looked back to the weird business of the Sign of Four, and the extraordinary circumstances connected with the Study in Scarlet, I felt that it would be a strange tangle indeed which he could not unravel.

I left him then, with the conviction that when I came again on the next evening I would find that he held in his hands all the clues which would lead up to the identity of the disappearing bridegroom of Miss Mary Sutherland.

A professional case of great gravity was engaging my own attention at the time, and the whole of next day I was busy at the bedside of the sufferer. It was not until close upon six o'clock that I found myself free and was able to spring into a carriage and drive to Baker Street, half afraid that I might be too late to assist at the dénouement of the little mystery. I found Sherlock Holmes alone, however, half asleep, with his long, thin form curled up in the recesses of his armchair. A formidable array of bottles and test-tubes, with the pungent cleanly smell of hydrochloric acid, told me that he had spent his day in the chemical work which was so dear to him.

"Well, have you solved it?" I asked as I entered.

"Yes. It was the bisulphate of baryta."

"No, no, the *mystery*!" I cried.

"Oh, that! I thought of the salt that I have been working upon. There was never any mystery in the matter, though, as I said yesterday, some of the details are of interest. The only drawback is that there is no law, I fear, that can touch the scoundrel."

"Who was he, then, and what was his object in deserting Miss Sutherland?"

The question was hardly out of my mouth, and Holmes had not yet opened his lips to reply, when we heard a heavy footfall in the passage and a tap at the door.

"This is the girl's stepfather, Mr. James Windibank," said Holmes. "He has written to me to say that he would be here at six. Come in!"

The man who entered was a sturdy, middle-sized fellow, some thirty years of age, clean-shaven, and sallow-skinned, with a bland, insinuating manner, and a pair of wonderfully sharp and penetrating grey eyes. He shot a questioning glance at each of us, placed his shiny top-hat upon the sideboard, and with a slight bow sidled down into the nearest chair.

"Good-evening, Mr. James Windibank," said Holmes. "I think that this typewritten letter is from you, in which you made an appointment with me for six o'clock?"

"Yes, sir. I am afraid that I am a little late, but I am not quite my own master, you know. I am sorry that Miss Sutherland has troubled you about this little matter, for I think it is far better not to wash linen of the sort in public. It was quite against my wishes that she came, but she is a very excitable, impulsive girl, as you may have noticed, and she is not easily controlled when she has made up her mind on a point. Of course, I did not mind you so much, as you are not connected with the official police, but it is not pleasant to have a family misfortune like this noised abroad. Besides, it is a useless expense, for how could you possibly find this Hosmer Angel?"

"On the contrary," said Holmes quietly, "I have every reason to believe that I will succeed in discovering Mr. Hosmer Angel."

Mr. Windibank gave a violent start and dropped his gloves. "I am delighted to hear it," he said.

"It is a curious thing," remarked Holmes, "that a typewriter has really quite as much individuality as a man's handwriting. Unless they are quite new, no two of them write exactly alike. Some letters get more worn than others, and some wear only on one side. Now, you remark in this note of yours, Mr. Windibank, that in every case there is some little slurring over of the 'e,' and a slight defect in the tail of the 'r.' There are fourteen other characteristics, but those are the more obvious."

"We do all our correspondence with this machine at the office, and no doubt it is a little worn," our visitor answered, glancing keenly at Holmes with his bright little eyes.

"And now I will show you what is really a very interesting study, Mr. Windibank," Holmes continued. "I think of writing another little monograph some of these days on the typewriter and its relation to crime. It is a subject to which I have devoted some little attention. I have here four letters which purport to come from the missing man. They are all typewritten. In each case, not only are the 'e's' slurred and the 'r's' tailless, but you will observe, if you care to use my magnifying lens, that the fourteen other characteristics to which I have alluded are there as well."

Mr. Windibank sprang out of his chair and picked up his hat. "I cannot waste time over this sort of fantastic talk, Mr. Holmes," he said. "If you can catch the man, catch him, and let me know when you have done it."

"Certainly," said Holmes, stepping over and turning the key in the door. "I let you know, then, that I have caught him!"

"What! Where?!" shouted Mr. Windibank, turning white to his lips and glancing about him like a rat in a trap.

"Oh, it won't do—really it won't," said Holmes suavely. "There is no possible getting out of it, Mr. Windibank. It is quite too transparent, and it was a very bad compliment when you said that it was impossible for me to solve so simple a question. That's right! Sit down and let us talk it over."

Our visitor collapsed into a chair, with a ghastly face and a glitter of moisture on his brow. "It—it's not actionable," he stammered.

"I am very much afraid that it is not. But between ourselves, Windibank, it was as cruel and selfish and heartless a trick in a petty way as ever came before me. Now, let me just run over the course of events, and you will contradict me if I go wrong."

The man sat huddled up in his chair, with his

head sunk upon his chest, like one who is utterly crushed.  Holmes stuck his feet up on the corner of the mantelpiece and, leaning back with his hands in his pockets, began talking, rather to himself, as it seemed, than to us.

"The man married a woman very much older than himself for her money," he said, "and he enjoyed the use of the money of the daughter as long as she lived with them.  It was a considerable sum, for people in their position, and the loss of it would have made a serious difference.  It was worth an effort to preserve it.  The daughter was of a good, amiable disposition, but affectionate and warm-hearted in her ways, so that it was evident that with her fair personal advantages, and her little income, she would not be allowed to remain single long.  Now her marriage would mean, of course, the loss of a hundred a year, so what does her stepfather do to prevent it?  He takes the obvious course of keeping her at home and forbidding her to seek the company of people of her own age.  But soon he found that that would not answer forever.  She became restive, insisted upon her rights, and finally announced her positive intention of going to a certain ball.  What does her clever stepfather do then?  He conceives an idea more creditable to his head than to his heart.  With the connivance and assistance of his wife he disguised himself, covered those keen eyes with tinted glasses, masked the face with a moustache and a pair of bushy whiskers, sunk that clear voice into an insinuating whisper, and doubly secure on account of the girl's short sight, he appears as Mr. Hosmer Angel, and keeps off other lovers by making love himself."

"It was only a joke at first," groaned our visitor.

"We never thought that she would have been so carried away!"

"Very likely not. However that may be, the young lady was very decidedly carried away, and, having quite made up her mind that her stepfather was in France, the suspicion of treachery never for an instant entered her mind. She was flattered by the gentleman's attentions, and the effect was increased by the loudly expressed admiration of her mother. Then Mr. Angel began to call, for it was obvious that the matter should be pushed as far as it would go if a real effect were to be produced. There were meetings, and an engagement, which would finally secure the girl's affections from turning towards anyone else. But the deception could not be kept up forever. These pretended journeys to France were rather cumbersome. The thing to do was clearly to bring the business to an end in such a dramatic manner that it would leave a permanent impression upon the young lady's mind and prevent her from looking upon any other suitor for some time to come. Hence those vows of fidelity exacted upon a Testament, and hence also the allusions to a possibility of something happening on the very morning of the wedding. James Windibank wished Miss Sutherland to be so bound to Hosmer Angel, and so uncertain as to his fate, that for ten years to come, at any rate, she would not listen to another man. As far as the church door he brought her, and then, as he could go no farther, he conveniently vanished away by the old trick of stepping in at one door of a four-wheeler and out at the other. I think that was the chain of events, Mr. Windibank!"

Our visitor had recovered something of his assurance while Holmes had been talking, and he rose from his chair now with a cold sneer upon his pale face.

"It may be so, or it may not, Mr. Holmes," he said, "but if you are so very sharp, you ought to be sharp enough to know that it is you who are breaking the law now, and not me. I have done nothing actionable from the first, but as long as you keep that door locked you lay yourself open to an action for assault and illegal constraint."

"The law cannot, as you say, touch you," said Holmes, unlocking and throwing open the door, "yet there never was a man who deserved punishment more. If the young lady has a brother or a friend, he ought to lay a whip across your shoulders. By Jove!" he continued, flushing up at the sight of the bitter sneer upon the man's face, "it is not part of my duties to my client, but here's a hunting crop handy, and I think I shall just treat myself to—" He took two swift steps to the whip, but before he could grasp it, there was a wild clatter of steps upon the stairs, the heavy hall door banged, and from the window we could see Mr. James Windibank running at the top of his speed down the road.

"There's a cold-blooded scoundrel!" said Holmes, laughing, as he threw himself down into his chair once more. "That fellow will rise from crime to crime until he does something very bad, and ends on a gallows. The case has, in some respects, been not entirely devoid of interest."

"I cannot now entirely see all the steps of your reasoning," I remarked.

"Well, of course it was obvious from the first that this Mr. Hosmer Angel must have some strong object for his curious conduct, and it was equally clear that the only man who really profited by the incident, as far as we could see, was the stepfather.  Then the fact that the two men were never together, but that the one always appeared when the other was away, was suggestive.  So were the tinted spectacles and the curious voice, which both hinted at a disguise, as did the bushy whiskers.  My suspicions were all confirmed by his peculiar action in typewriting his signature, which, of course, inferred that his handwriting was so familiar to her that she would recognize even the smallest sample of it.  You see all these isolated facts, together with many minor ones, all pointed in the same direction."

"And how did you verify them?"

"Having once spotted my man, it was easy to get corroboration.  I knew the firm for which this man worked.  Having taken the printed description, I eliminated everything from it which could be the result of a disguise—the whiskers, the glasses, the voice, and I sent it to the firm, with a request that they would inform me whether it answered to the description of any of their travelers.  I had already noticed the peculiarities of the typewriter, and I wrote to the man himself at his business address asking him if he would come here.  As I expected, his reply was typewritten and revealed the same trivial but characteristic defects.  The same post brought me a letter from Westhouse & Marbank, of Fenchurch Street, to say that the description tallied in every respect with that of their employee, James Windibank.  *Voil tout*!"

"And Miss Sutherland?"

"If I tell her, she will not believe me.  You may remember the old Persian saying: 'There is danger for him who taketh the tiger cub, and danger also for whoso snatches a delusion from a woman.'  There is as much sense in Hafiz as in Horace, and as much knowledge of the world."

# 4th ADVENTURE!
# THE BOSCOMBE VALLEY MYSTERY

We were seated at breakfast one morning, my wife and I, when the maid brought in a telegram.  It was from Sherlock Holmes and ran in this way:

"Have you a couple of days to spare?  Have just been wired for from the west of England in connection with Boscombe Valley tragedy.  Shall be glad if you will come with me.  Air and scenery perfect.  Leave Paddington by the 11:15."

"What do you say, dear?" said my wife, looking across at me.  "Will you go?"

"I really don't know what to say.  I have a fairly long list at present."

"Oh, Anstruther would do your work for you.  You have been looking a little pale lately.  I think that the change would do you good, and you are always so interested in Mr. Sherlock Holmes' cases."

"I should be ungrateful if I were not, seeing what I gained through one of them," I answered.  "But if I am to go, I must pack at once, for I have only half an hour."

My experience of camp life in Afghanistan had at least had the effect of making me a prompt and ready traveler.  My wants were few and simple, so that in less than the time stated I was in a cab with my valise, rattling away to Paddington Station. Sherlock Holmes was pacing up and down the platform, his tall, gaunt figure made even gaunter and taller by his long grey traveling-cloak and close-fitting cloth cap.

"It is really very good of you to come, Watson," he said. "It makes a considerable difference to me, having someone with me on whom I can thoroughly rely. Local aid is always either worthless or else biased. If you will keep the two corner seats, I shall get the tickets."

We had the carriage to ourselves save for an immense litter of papers which Holmes had brought with him. Among these he rummaged and read, with intervals of note-taking and of meditation, until we were past Reading. Then he suddenly rolled them all into a gigantic ball and tossed them up onto the rack.

"Have you heard anything of the case?" he asked.

"Not a word. I have not seen a paper for some days."

"The London press has not had very full accounts. I have just been looking through all the recent papers in order to master the particulars. It seems, from what I gather, to be one of those simple cases which are so extremely difficult."

"That sounds a little paradoxical."

"But it is profoundly true. Singularity is almost invariably a clue. The more featureless and commonplace a crime is, the more difficult it is to bring it home. In this case, however, they have established a very serious case against the son of the murdered man."

"It is a murder, then?"

"Well, it is conjectured to be so. I shall take nothing for granted until I have the opportunity of looking personally into it. I will explain the state of things to you, as far as I have been able to understand it, in a very few words.

"Boscombe Valley is a country district not very far from Ross, in Herefordshire. The largest landed proprietor in that part is a Mr. John Turner, who made his money in Australia and returned some years ago to the old country. One of the farms which he held, that of Hatherley, was rented to Mr. Charles McCarthy, who was also an ex-Australian. The men had known each other in the colonies, so that it was not unnatural that when they came to settle down they should do so as near each other as possible. Turner was apparently the richer man, so McCarthy became his tenant but still remained, it seems, upon terms of perfect equality, as they were frequently together. McCarthy had one son, a lad of eighteen, and Turner had an only daughter of the same age, but neither of them had wives living. They appear to have avoided the society of the neighboring English families and to have led retired lives, though both the McCarthys were fond of sport and were frequently seen at the race-meetings of the neighborhood. McCarthy kept two servants—a man and a girl. Turner had a considerable household, some half-dozen at the least. That is as much as I have been able to gather about the families. Now for the facts.

"On June 3rd—that is, on Monday last—McCarthy left his house at Hatherley about three in the afternoon and walked down to the Boscombe Pool, which is a small lake formed by the spreading out of the stream which runs down the Boscombe Valley. He had been out with his serving-man in the morning at Ross, and he had told the man that he must hurry, as he had an appointment of importance to keep at three. From that appointment, he never came back alive.

"From Hatherley Farm-house to the Boscombe Pool is a quarter of a mile, and two people saw him as he passed over this ground. One was an old woman, whose name is not mentioned, and the other was William Crowder, a game-keeper in the employ of Mr. Turner. Both these witnesses depose that Mr. McCarthy was walking alone. The game-keeper adds that, within a few minutes of his seeing Mr. McCarthy pass, he had seen the son, Mr. James McCarthy, going the same way with a gun under his arm. To the best of his belief, the father was actually in sight at the time, and the son was following him. He thought no more of the matter until he heard in the evening of the tragedy that had occurred.

"The two McCarthys were seen after the time when William Crowder, the game-keeper, lost sight of them. The Boscombe Pool is thickly wooded round, with just a fringe of grass and of reeds round the edge. A girl of fourteen, Patience Moran, who is the daughter of the lodge-keeper of the Boscombe Valley estate, was in one of the woods picking flowers. She states that while she was there she saw, at the border of the wood and close by the lake, Mr. McCarthy and his son, and that they appeared to be having a violent quarrel. She heard the elder McCarthy using very strong language to his son, and she saw the latter raise up his hand as if to strike his father. She was so frightened by their violence that she ran away and told her mother when she reached home that she had left the two McCarthys quarreling near Boscombe Pool, and that she was afraid that they were going to fight.  She had hardly said the words when young Mr. McCarthy came running up to the lodge to say that he had found his father dead in the wood, and to ask for the help of the lodge-keeper.  He was much excited, without either his gun or his hat, and his right hand and sleeve were observed to be stained with fresh blood.  On following him, they found the dead body stretched out upon the grass beside the pool.  The head had been beaten in by repeated blows of some heavy and blunt weapon.  The injuries were such as might very well have been inflicted by the butt-end of his son's gun, which was found lying on the grass within a few paces of the body.  Under these circumstances, the young man was instantly arrested, and a verdict of 'wilful murder' having been returned at the inquest on Tuesday, he was on Wednesday brought before the magistrates at Ross, who have referred the case to the next Assizes.  Those are the main facts of the case as they came out before the coroner and the police-court."

"I could hardly imagine a more damning case," I remarked. "If ever circumstantial evidence pointed to a criminal, it does so here."

"Circumstantial evidence is a very tricky thing," answered Holmes thoughtfully. "It may seem to point very straight to one thing, but if you shift your own point of view a little, you may find it pointing in an equally uncompromising manner to something entirely different. It must be confessed, however, that the case looks exceedingly grave against the young man, and it is very possible that he is indeed the culprit.   There are several people in the neighborhood, however, and among them Miss Turner, the daughter of the neighboring landowner, who believe in his innocence, and who have retained Lestrade, whom you may recollect in connection with the Study in Scarlet, to work out the case in his interest. Lestrade, being rather puzzled, has referred the case to me, and hence it is that two middle-aged gentlemen are flying westward at fifty miles an hour instead of quietly digesting their breakfasts at home."

"I am afraid," I said, "that the facts are so obvious that you will find little credit to be gained out of this case."

"There is nothing more deceptive than an obvious fact," he answered, laughing. "Besides, we may chance to hit upon some other 'obvious facts' which may have been by no means obvious to Mr. Lestrade. You know me too well to think that I am boasting when I say that I shall either confirm or destroy his theory by means which he is quite incapable of employing, or even of understanding. To take the first example to hand, I very clearly perceive that in your bedroom the window is upon the right-hand side, and yet I question whether Mr. Lestrade would have noted even so self-evident a thing as that."

"How on earth—?"

"My dear fellow, I know you well. I know the military neatness which characterizes you. You shave every morning, and in this season you shave by the sunlight; but since your shaving is less and less complete as we get farther back on the left side, until it becomes positively slovenly as we get round the angle of the jaw, it is surely very clear that that side is less illuminated than the other. I could not imagine a man of your habits looking at himself in an equal light and being satisfied with such a result. I only quote this as a trivial example of observation and inference. Therein lies my specialty, and it is just possible that it may be of some service in the investigation which lies before us. There are one or two minor points which were brought out in the inquest, and which are worth considering."

"What are they?"

"It appears that his arrest did not take place at once, but after the return to Hatherley Farm. On the inspector of constabulary informing him that he was a prisoner, he remarked that he was not surprised to hear it, and that it was no more than his desserts. This observation of his had the natural effect of removing any traces of doubt which might have remained in the minds of the coroner's jury."

"It was a confession!" I exclaimed.

"No, for it was followed by a protestation of innocence."

"Coming on the top of such a damning series of events, it was at least a most suspicious remark."

"On the contrary," said Holmes, "it is the brightest rift which I can at present see in the clouds. However innocent he might be, he could not be such an absolute imbecile as not to see that the circumstances were very black against him. Had he appeared surprised at his own arrest, or feigned indignation at it, I should have looked upon it as highly suspicious, because such surprise or anger would not be natural under the circumstances, and yet might appear to be the best policy to a scheming man. His frank acceptance of the situation marks him as either an innocent man, or else as a man of considerable self-restraint and firmness. As to his remark about his desserts, it was also not unnatural if you consider that he stood beside the dead body of his father, and that there is no doubt that he had that very day so far forgotten his filial duty as to bandy words with him, and even, according to the little girl whose evidence is so important, to raise his hand as if to strike him. The self-reproach and contrition which are displayed in his remark appear to me to be the signs of a healthy mind rather than of a guilty one."

I shook my head. "Many men have been hanged on far slighter evidence," I remarked.

"So they have. And many men have been wrongfully hanged."

"What is the young man's own account of the matter?"

"It is, I am afraid, not very encouraging to his supporters, though there are one or two points in it which are suggestive. You will find it here, and may read it for yourself."

He picked out from his bundle a copy of the local Herefordshire paper, and having turned down the sheet, he pointed out the paragraph in which the unfortunate young man had given his own statement of what had occurred. I settled myself down in the corner of the carriage and read it very carefully. It ran in this way:

"Mr. James McCarthy, the only son of the deceased, was then called and gave evidence as follows: 'I had been away from home for three days at Bristol, and had only just returned upon the morning of last Monday, the 3rd. My father was absent from home at the time of my arrival, and I was informed by the maid that he had driven over to Ross with John Cobb, the groom. Shortly after my return, I heard the wheels of his trap in the yard, and, looking out of my window, I saw him get out and walk rapidly out of the yard, though I was not aware in which direction he was going.  I then took my gun and strolled out in the direction of the Boscombe Pool, with the intention of visiting the rabbit warren which is upon the other side.  On my way, I saw William Crowder, the game-keeper, as he had stated in his evidence; but he is mistaken in thinking that I was following my father.  I had no idea that he was in front of me.  When about a hundred yards from the pool, I heard a cry of "Cooee!" which was a usual signal between my father and myself!  I then hurried forward, and found him standing by the pool.  He appeared to be much surprised at seeing me, and asked me rather roughly what I was doing there.  A conversation ensued which led to high words and almost to blows, for my father was a man of a very violent temper.  Seeing that his passion was becoming ungovernable, I left him and returned towards Hatherley Farm.  I had not gone more than 150 yards, however, when I heard a hideous outcry behind me, which caused me to run back again.  I found my father expiring upon the ground, with his head terribly injured.  I dropped my gun and held him in my arms, but he almost instantly expired.  I knelt beside him for some minutes, and then made my way to Mr. Turner's lodge-keeper, his house being the nearest, to ask for assistance.  I saw no one near my father when I returned, and I have no idea how he came by his injuries.  He was not a popular man, being somewhat cold and forbidding in his manners, but he had, as far as I know, no active enemies.  I know nothing further of the matter.'

"The Coroner: Did your father make any statement to you before he died?

"Witness: He mumbled a few words, but I could only catch some allusion to a rat.

"The Coroner: What did you understand by that?

"Witness: It conveyed no meaning to me.  I thought that he was delirious.

"The Coroner: What was the point upon which you and your father had this final quarrel?

"Witness: I should prefer not to answer.

"The Coroner: I am afraid that I must press it.

"Witness: It is really impossible for me to tell you. I can assure you that it has nothing to do with the sad tragedy which followed.

"The Coroner: That is for the court to decide.  I need not point out to you that your refusal to answer will prejudice your case considerably in any future proceedings which may arise.

"Witness: I must still refuse.

"The Coroner: I understand that the cry of 'Cooee' was a common signal between you and your father?

"Witness: It was.

"The Coroner: How was it, then, that he uttered it before he saw you, and before he even knew that you had returned from Bristol?

"Witness (with considerable confusion): I do not know.

"A Juryman: Did you see nothing which aroused your suspicions when you returned on hearing the cry and found your father fatally injured?

"Witness: Nothing definite.

"The Coroner: What do you mean?

"Witness: I was so disturbed and excited as I rushed out into the open, that I could think of nothing except of my father.  Yet I have a vague impression that as I ran forward something lay upon the ground to the left of me.  It seemed to me to be something grey in color, a coat of some sort, or a plaid perhaps.

When I rose from my father I looked round for it, but it was gone.

"'Do you mean that it disappeared before you went for help?'

"'Yes, it was gone.'

"'You cannot say what it was?'

"'No, I just had a feeling something was there.'

"'How far from the body?'

"'A dozen yards or so.'

"'And how far from the edge of the wood?'

"'About the same.'

"'Then, if it was removed, it was while you were within a dozen yards of it?'

"'Yes, but with my back towards it.'

"This concluded the examination of the witness."

"I see," said I as I glanced down the column, "that the coroner in his concluding remarks was rather severe upon young McCarthy.  He calls attention, and with reason, to the discrepancy about his father having signaled to him before seeing him, also to his refusal to give details of his conversation with his father, and his singular account of his father's dying words.  They are all, as he remarks, very much against the son."

Holmes laughed softly to himself and stretched himself out upon the cushioned seat. "Both you and the coroner have been at some pains," he said, "to single out the very strongest points in the young man's favor.  Don't you see that you alternately give him credit for having too much imagination and too little?  Too little, if he could not invent a cause of quarrel which would give him the sympathy of the jury; too much, if he evolved from his own inner consciousness anything so bizarre as a dying reference to a rat, and the incident of the vanishing cloth. No, sir, I shall approach this case from the point of view that what this young man says is true, and we shall see to where that hypothesis will lead us. Not another word shall I say of this case until we are on the scene of action. We lunch at Swindon, and I see that we shall be there in twenty minutes."

It was nearly four o'clock when we at last—after passing through the beautiful Stroud Valley and over the broad gleaming Severn—found ourselves at the pretty little country-town of Ross. A lean, ferret-like man, furtive and sly-looking, was waiting for us upon the platform. In spite of the light brown dustcoat and leather-leggings which he wore in deference to his rustic surroundings, I had no difficulty in recognizing Lestrade of Scotland Yard. With him, we drove to the Hereford Arms where a room had already been engaged for us.

"I have ordered a carriage," said Lestrade as we sat over a cup of tea. "I knew your energetic nature, and that you would not be happy until you had been on the scene of the crime."

"It was very nice and complimentary of you," Holmes answered. "It is entirely a question of barometric pressure."

Lestrade looked startled. "I do not quite follow," he said.

"How is the barometer? Twenty-nine, I see. No wind, and not a cloud in the sky. I do not think that it is probable that I shall use the carriage tonight."

Lestrade laughed indulgently. "You have, no doubt, already formed your conclusions from the newspapers," he said. "The case is as plain as a pikestaff, and the more one goes into it, the plainer it becomes. Still, of course, one can't refuse a lady, and such a very positive one, too. She has heard of you, and would have your opinion, though I repeatedly told her that there was nothing which you could do which I had not already done. Why, bless my soul! Here is her carriage at the door."

He had hardly spoken before there rushed into the room one of the most lovely young women that I have ever seen in my life! Her violet eyes shining, her lips parted, a pink flush upon her cheeks, all thought of her natural reserve lost in her overpowering excitement and concern.

"Oh, Mr. Sherlock Holmes!" she cried, glancing from one to the other of us, and finally, with a woman's quick intuition, fastening upon my companion. "I am so glad that you have come! I have driven down to tell you so—I know that James didn't do it! I know it, and I want you to start upon your work knowing it, too. Never let yourself doubt upon that point. We have known each other since we were little children, and I know his faults as no one else does; but he is too tender-hearted to hurt a fly. Such a charge is absurd to anyone who really knows him!"

"I hope we may clear him, Miss Turner," said Sherlock Holmes. "You may rely upon my doing all that I can."

"But you have read the evidence. You have formed some conclusion? Do you not see some loophole, some flaw? Do you not yourself think that he is innocent?"

"I think that it is very probable."

"There, now!" she cried, throwing back her head and looking defiantly at Lestrade. "You hear! He gives me hopes."

Lestrade shrugged his shoulders. "I am afraid that my colleague has been a little quick in forming his conclusions," he said.

"But he is right.  Oh!  I know that he is right. James never did it.  And about his quarrel with his father, I am sure that the reason why he would not speak about it to the coroner was because *I* was concerned in it!"

"In what way?" asked Holmes.

"It is no time for me to hide anything. James and his father had many disagreements about me.  Mr. McCarthy was very anxious that there should be a marriage between us.  James and I have always loved each other as brother and sister; but of course. he is young and has seen very little of life yet, and—and—well, he naturally did not wish to do anything like that yet.  So there were quarrels, and this, I am sure, was one of them."

"And your father?" asked Holmes.  "Was he in favor of such a union?"

"No, he was averse to it also.  No one but Mr. McCarthy was in favor of it."  A quick blush passed over her fresh young face as Holmes shot one of his keen, questioning glances at her.

"Thank you for this information," he said.  "May I see your father if I call tomorrow?"

"I am afraid the doctor won't allow it."

"The doctor?"

"Yes, have you not heard? Poor father has never been strong for years back, but this has broken him down completely.  He has taken to his bed, and Dr. Willows says that he is a wreck and that his nervous system is shattered. Mr. McCarthy was the only man alive who had known dad in the old days in Victoria."

"Ha! In Victoria! That is important."

"Yes, at the mines."

"Quite so; at the gold-mines, where, as I

understand, Mr. Turner made his money."

"Yes, certainly."

"Thank you, Miss Turner.  You have been of material assistance to me."

"You will tell me if you have any news tomorrow. No doubt you will go to the prison to see James. Oh, if you do, Mr. Holmes, do tell him that I *know* him to be innocent!"

"I will, Miss Turner."

"I must go home now, for dad is very ill, and he misses me so if I leave him. Goodbye, and God help you in your undertaking." She hurried from the room as impulsively as she had entered, and we heard the wheels of her carriage rattle off down the street.

"I am ashamed of you, Holmes," said Lestrade with dignity after a few minutes' silence. "Why should you raise up hopes which you are bound to disappoint?  I am not over-tender of heart, but I call it *cruel!*"

"I think that I see my way to clearing James McCarthy," said Holmes. "Have you an order to see him in prison?"

"Yes, but only for you and me."

"Then I shall reconsider my resolution about going out.  We have still time to take a train to Hereford and see him tonight?"

"Ample."

"Then let us do so.  Watson, I fear that you will find it very slow, but I shall only be away a couple of hours."

I walked down to the station with them, and then wandered through the streets of the little town, finally returning to the hotel, where I lay upon the sofa and tried to interest myself in a yellow-backed novel. The puny plot of the story was so thin, however, when compared to the deep mystery through which we were groping, and I found my attention wander so continually from the action to the fact, that I at last flung it across the room and gave myself up entirely to a consideration of the events of the day.

Supposing that this unhappy young man's story were absolutely true, then what hellish thing, what absolutely unforeseen and extraordinary calamity could have occurred between the time when he parted from his father ... and the moment when, drawn back by his screams, he rushed into the glade? It was something terrible and deadly! What could it be? Might not the nature of the injuries reveal something to my medical instincts?

I rang the bell and called for the weekly county paper, which contained a verbatim account of the inquest. In the surgeon's deposition, it was stated that the posterior third of the left parietal bone and the left half of the occipital bone had been shattered by a heavy blow from a blunt weapon. I marked the spot upon my own head. Clearly such a blow must have been struck from behind! That was to some extent in favor of the accused, as when seen quarreling he was face-to-face with his father. Still, it did not go for very much, for the older man might have turned his back before the blow fell. Still, it might be worthwhile to call Holmes' attention to it. Then there was the peculiar dying reference to a rat. What could that mean? It could not be delirium. A man dying from a sudden blow does not commonly become delirious. No, it was more likely to be an attempt to explain how he met his fate. But what could it indicate? I cudgeled my brains to find some possible explanation. And then the incident of the grey cloth seen by young McCarthy. If that were true, the murderer must have dropped some part of his clothing—presumably his overcoat—in his flight, and must have had the hardihood to return and to carry it away at the instant when the son was kneeling with his back turned not a dozen paces off. What a tissue of mysteries and improbabilities the whole thing was! I did not wonder at Lestrade's opinion, and yet I had so much faith in Sherlock Holmes' insight that I could not lose hope as long as every fresh fact seemed to strengthen his conviction of young McCarthy's innocence.

It was late before Sherlock Holmes returned. He came back alone, for Lestrade was staying in lodgings in the town.

"The barometer still keeps very high," he remarked as he sat down. "It is of importance that it should not rain before we are able to go over the ground! On the other hand, a man should be at his very best and keenest for such nice work as that, and I did not wish to do it when fatigued by a long journey. I have seen young McCarthy."

"And what did you learn from him?"

"Nothing."

"Could he throw no light?"

"None at all. I was inclined to think at one time that he knew who had done it and was screening him or her, but I am convinced now that he is as puzzled as everyone else. He is not a very quick-witted youth, though handsome and, I should think, sound at heart."

"I cannot admire his taste," I remarked, "if it is indeed a fact that he was averse to a marriage with so charming a young lady as this Miss Turner!"

"Ah, thereby hangs a rather painful tale. This fellow is madly, insanely, in love with her, but some two years ago, when he was only a lad, and before he really knew her—for she had been away five years at a boarding-school—what does the idiot do but get into the clutches of a barmaid in Bristol and marry her at a registry office?  No one knows a word of the matter, but you can imagine how maddening it must be to him to be upbraided for not doing what he would give his very eyes to do, but what he knows to be absolutely impossible.  It was sheer frenzy of this sort which made him throw his hands up into the air when his father, at their last interview, was goading him on to propose to Miss Turner.  On the other hand, he had no means of supporting himself, and his father, who was by all accounts a very hard man, would have thrown him over utterly had he known the truth.  It was with his barmaid wife that he had spent the last three days in Bristol, and his father did not know where he was.  Mark that point—it is of importance!  Good has come out of evil, however, for the barmaid, finding from the papers that he is in serious trouble and likely to be hanged, has thrown him over utterly and has written to him to say that she has a husband already in the Bermuda Dockyard, so that there is really no tie between them.  I think that that bit of news has consoled young McCarthy for all that he has suffered."

"But if he is innocent, who has done it?"

"Ah!  Who?  I would call your attention very particularly to two points:  One is that the murdered man had an appointment with someone at the pool, and that the someone could not have been his son, for his son was away, and he did not know when he would return; the second is that the murdered man was heard to cry 'Cooee!' before he knew that his son had returned.  Those are the crucial points upon which the case depends!  And now let us talk about George Meredith, if you please, and we shall leave all minor matters until tomorrow."

There was no rain, as Holmes had foretold, and the morning broke bright and cloudless.  At nine o'clock, Lestrade called for us with the carriage, and we set off for Hatherley Farm and the Boscombe Pool.

"There is serious news this morning," Lestrade observed.  "It is said that Mr. Turner, of the Hall, is so ill that his life is despaired of."

"An elderly man, I presume?" said Holmes.

"About sixty; but his constitution has been shattered by his life abroad, and he has been in failing health for some time.  This business has had a very bad effect upon him.  He was an old friend of McCarthy's, and, I may add, a great benefactor to him, for I have learned that he gave him Hatherley Farm rent free."

"Indeed!  That is interesting," said Holmes.

"Oh, yes!  In a hundred other ways he has helped him.  Everybody about here speaks of his kindness to him."

"Really!  Does it not strike you as a little singular that this McCarthy, who appears to have had little of his own, and to have been under such obligations to Turner, should still talk of marrying his son to Turner's daughter, who is, presumably, heiress to the estate, and that in such a very cocksure manner, as if it were merely a case of a proposal and all else would follow?  It is the more strange, since we know that Turner himself was averse to the idea.  The daughter told us as much.  Do you not deduce something from that?"

"We have got to the deductions and the

inferences," said Lestrade, winking at me. "I find it hard enough to tackle facts, Holmes, without flying away after theories and fancies."

"You are right," said Holmes demurely; "you do find it very hard to tackle the facts."

"Anyhow, I have grasped one fact which you seem to find it difficult to get hold of," replied Lestrade with some warmth.

"And that is—?"

"That McCarthy senior met his death from McCarthy junior, and that all theories to the contrary are the merest moonshine!"

"Well, moonshine is a brighter thing than fog," said Holmes, laughing. "But I am very much mistaken if this is not Hatherley Farm upon the left."

"Yes, that is it." It was a widespread, comfortable-looking building, two-storied, slate-roofed, with great yellow blotches of lichen upon the grey walls. The drawn blinds and the smokeless chimneys, however, gave it a stricken look, as though the weight of this horror still lay heavy upon it. We called at the door, when the maid, at Holmes' request, showed us the boots which her master wore at the time of his death, and also a pair of the son's, though not the pair which he had then had. Having measured these very carefully from seven or eight different points, Holmes desired to be led to the court-yard, from which we all followed the winding track which led to Boscombe Pool.

Sherlock Holmes was transformed when he was hot upon such a scent as this. Men who had only known the quiet thinker and logician of Baker Street would have failed to recognize him. His face flushed and darkened. His brows were drawn into two hard black lines, while his eyes shone out from beneath them with a steely glitter. His face was bent downward, his shoulders bowed, his lips compressed, and the veins stood out like whipcord in his long, sinewy neck. His nostrils seemed to dilate with a purely animal lust for the chase, and his mind was so absolutely concentrated upon the matter before him that a question or remark fell unheeded upon his ears, or, at the most, only provoked a quick, impatient snarl in reply.

Swiftly and silently, he made his way along the track which ran through the meadows, and so by way of the woods to the Boscombe Pool. It was damp, marshy ground, as is all that district, and there were marks of many feet, both upon the path and amid the short grass which bounded it on either side. Sometimes Holmes would hurry on, sometimes stop dead, and once he made quite a little detour into the meadow. Lestrade and I walked behind him, the detective indifferent and contemptuous, while I watched my friend with the interest which sprang from the conviction that every one of his actions was directed towards a definite end.

The Boscombe Pool, which is a little reed-girt sheet of water some fifty yards across, is situated at the boundary between the Hatherley Farm and the private park of the wealthy Mr. Turner. Above the woods which lined it upon the farther side we could see the red, jutting pinnacles which marked the site of the rich landowner's dwelling. On the Hatherley side of the pool the woods grew very thick, and there was a narrow belt of sodden grass twenty paces across between the edge of the trees and the reeds which lined the lake. Lestrade showed us the exact spot at which the body had been found, and, indeed, so moist was the ground, that I could plainly see the traces which had been left by the fall of the stricken man.  To Holmes, as I could see by his eager face and peering eyes, very many other things were to be read upon the trampled grass.  He ran round, like a dog who is picking up a scent, and then turned upon my companion.

"What did you go into the pool for?" he asked.

"I fished about with a rake.  I thought there might be some weapon or other trace.  But how on earth—"

"Oh, tut, tut!  I have no time!  That left foot of yours with its inward twist is all over the place.  A mole could trace it, and there it vanishes among the reeds.  Oh, how simple it would all have been had I been here before they came like a herd of buffalo and wallowed all over it.  Here is where the party with the lodge-keeper came, and they have covered all tracks for six or eight feet round the body.  But here are three separate tracks of the same feet."  He drew out a magnifying glass and lay down upon his waterproof to have a better view, talking all the time rather to himself than to us.  "These are young McCarthy's feet.  Twice he was walking, and once he ran swiftly, so that the soles are deeply marked and the heels hardly visible.  That bears out his story.  He ran when he saw his father on the ground.  Then here are the father's feet as he paced up and down.  What is this, then?  It is the butt-end of the gun as the son stood listening.  And this?  Ha, ha!  What have we here?  Tiptoes!  *Tiptoes*!  Square, too, quite unusual boots!  They come, they go, they come again—of course that was for the cloak.  Now where did they come from?"  He ran up and down, sometimes losing, sometimes finding the track until we were well within the edge of the wood and under the shadow of a great beech, the largest tree in the neighborhood.  Holmes traced his way to the farther side of this and lay down once more upon his face with a little cry of satisfaction.

For a long time he remained there, turning over the leaves and dried sticks, gathering up what seemed to me to be dust into an envelope and examining with his magnifying glass not only the ground but even the bark of the tree as far as he could reach.  A jagged stone was lying among the moss, and this also he carefully examined and retained.  Then he followed a pathway through the wood until he came to the highroad, where all traces were lost.

"It has been a case of considerable interest," he remarked, returning to his natural manner.  "I fancy that this grey house on the right must be the lodge. I think that I will go in and have a word with Moran, and perhaps write a little note. Having done that, we may drive back to our luncheon.  You may walk to the cab, and I shall be with you presently."

It was about ten minutes before we regained our cab and drove back into Ross, Holmes still carrying with him the stone which he had picked up in the wood.

"This may interest you, Lestrade," he remarked, holding it out.  "The murder was done with it."

"I see no marks."

"There are none."

"How do you know, then?"

"The grass was growing under it.  It had only lain there a few days.  There was no sign of a place whence it had been taken.  It corresponds with the injuries.  There is no sign of any other weapon."

"And the murderer?"

"Is a tall man, left-handed, limps with the right

leg, wears thick-soled shooting-boots and a grey cloak, smokes Indian cigars, uses a cigar-holder, and carries a blunt pen-knife in his pocket. There are several other indications, but these may be enough to aid us in our search."

Lestrade laughed. "I am afraid that I am still a sceptic," he said. "Theories are all very well, but we have to deal with a hard-headed British jury."

"*We shall see what we shall see*," answered Holmes calmly in French. "You work your own method, and I shall work mine. I shall be busy this afternoon, and shall probably return to London by the evening train."

"And leave your case unfinished?"

"No, finished."

"But the mystery?"

"It is solved."

"Who was the criminal, then?"

"The gentleman I describe."

"But who is he?"

"Surely it would not be difficult to find out. This is not such a populous neighborhood."

Lestrade shrugged his shoulders. "I am a practical man," he said, "and I really cannot undertake to go about the country looking for a left-handed gentleman with a game leg. I should become the laughing-stock of Scotland Yard."

"All right," said Holmes quietly. "I have given you the chance. Here are your lodgings. Goodbye. I shall drop you a line before I leave."

Having left Lestrade at his rooms, we drove to our hotel, where we found lunch upon the table. Holmes was silent and buried in thought with a pained expression upon his face, as one who finds himself in a perplexing position.

"Look here, Watson," he said when the cloth was cleared "just sit down in this chair and let me preach to you for a little. I don't know quite what to do, and I should value your advice. Let me expound."

"Pray do so."

"Well, now, in considering this case there are two points about young McCarthy's narrative which struck us both instantly, although they impressed me in his favor and you against him. One was the fact that his father should, according to his account, cry 'Cooee!' before seeing him. The other was his singular dying reference to a rat. He mumbled several words, you understand, but that was all that caught the son's ear. Now from this double point our research must commence, and we will begin it by presuming that what the lad says is absolutely true."

"What of this 'Cooee!' then?"

"Well, obviously it could not have been meant for the son. The son, as far as he knew, was in Bristol. It was mere chance that he was within earshot. The 'Cooee!' was meant to attract the attention of whoever it was that he had the appointment with. But 'Cooee' is a distinctly *Australian* cry, and one which is used between Australians. There is a strong presumption that the person whom McCarthy expected to meet him at Boscombe Pool was someone who had been in Australia."

"What of the 'rat,' then?"

Sherlock Holmes took a folded paper from his pocket and flattened it out on the table. "This is a map of the Colony of Victoria," he said. "I wired to Bristol for it last night." He put his hand over part of the map. "What do you read?"

"*ARAT*," I read.

"And now?" He raised his hand.

*"BALLARAT."*

"Quite so. That was the word the man uttered, and of which his son only caught the last two syllables. He was trying to utter the name of his murderer. So and so, of Ballarat."

"It is wonderful!" I exclaimed.

"It is obvious. And now, you see, I had narrowed the field down considerably. The possession of a grey garment was a third point which, granting the son's statement to be correct, was a certainty. We have come now out of mere vagueness to the definite conception of an Australian from Ballarat with a grey cloak."

"Certainly."

"And one who was at home in the district, for the pool can only be approached by the farm or by the estate, where strangers could hardly wander."

"Quite so."

"Then comes our expedition of today. By an examination of the ground I gained the trifling details which I gave to that imbecile Lestrade, as to the personality of the criminal."

"But how did you gain them?"

"You know my method. It is founded upon the observation of trifles."

"His height I know that you might roughly judge from the length of his stride. His boots, too, might be told from their traces."

"Yes, they were peculiar boots."

"But his limp?"

"The impression of his right foot was always less distinct than his left. He put less weight upon it. Why? Because he limped—he was crippled."

"But his left-handedness?"

"You were yourself struck by the nature of the

injury as recorded by the surgeon at the inquest. The blow was struck from immediately behind, and yet was upon the left side. Now, how can that be unless it were by a left-handed man? He had stood behind that tree during the interview between the father and son. He had even smoked there. I found the ash of a cigar, which my special knowledge of tobacco ashes enables me to pronounce as an Indian cigar. I have, as you know, devoted some attention to this, and written a little monograph on the ashes of 140 different varieties of pipe, cigar, and cigarette tobacco. Having found the ash, I then looked round and discovered the stump among the moss where he had tossed it. It was an Indian cigar, of the variety which are rolled in Rotterdam."

"And the cigar-holder?"

"I could see that the end had not been in his mouth. Therefore he used a holder. The tip had been cut off, not bitten off, but the cut was not a clean one, so I deduced a blunt pen-knife."

"Holmes," I said, "you have drawn a net round this man from which he cannot escape, and you have saved an innocent human life as truly as if you had cut the cord which was hanging him. I see the direction in which all this points. The culprit is—"

"Mr. John Turner," cried the hotel waiter, opening the door of our sitting-room, and ushering in a visitor.

The man who entered was a strange and impressive figure. His slow, limping step and bowed shoulders gave the appearance of decrepitude, and yet his hard, deep-lined, craggy features, and his enormous limbs showed that he was possessed of unusual strength of body and of character. His tangled beard, grizzled hair, and outstanding, drooping eyebrows combined to give an air of dignity and power to his appearance, but his face was of an ashen white, while his lips and the corners of his nostrils were tinged with a shade of blue. It was clear to me at a glance that he was in the grip of some deadly and chronic disease.

"Please sit down on the sofa," said Holmes gently. "You had my note?"

"Yes, the lodge-keeper brought it up. You said that you wished to see me here to avoid scandal."

"I thought people would talk if I went to the Hall."

"And why did you wish to see me?" He looked across at my companion with despair in his weary eyes, as though his question was already answered.

"Yes," said Holmes, answering the look rather than the words. "It is so. I know all about McCarthy."

The old man sank his face in his hands. "God help me!" he cried. "But I would not have let the young man come to harm. I give you my word that I would have spoken out if it went against him at the Court of Assize."

"I am glad to hear you say so," said Holmes gravely.

"I would have spoken now had it not been for my dear girl. It would break her heart—it will break her heart when she hears that I am arrested."

"It may not come to that," said Holmes.

"What?"

"I am no official agent. I understand that it was your daughter who required my presence here, and I am acting in her interests. Young McCarthy must be got off, however."

"I am a dying man," said old Turner. "I have had diabetes for years. My doctor says it is a question whether I shall live a month. Yet I would rather die under my own roof than in jail."

Holmes rose and sat down at the table with his pen in his hand and a bundle of paper before him. "Just tell us the truth," he said. "I shall jot down the facts. You will sign it, and Watson here can witness it. Then I could produce your confession at the last extremity to save young McCarthy. I promise you that I shall not use it unless it is absolutely needed."

"It's as well," said the old man; "it's a question whether I shall live to the Assizes, so it matters little to me, but I should wish to spare Alice the shock. And now I will make the thing clear to you; it has been a long time in the acting, but will not take me long to tell.

"You didn't know this dead man, McCarthy. He was a devil incarnate! I tell you that! God keep you out of the clutches of such a man as he. His grip has been upon me these twenty years, and he has blasted my life. I'll tell you first how I came to be in his power.

"It was in the early '60's at the diggings. I was a young chap then, hot-blooded and reckless, ready to turn my hand at anything; I got among bad companions, took to drink, had no luck with my claim, took to the bush, and in a word became what you would call over here a 'highway robber'. There were six of us, and we had a wild, free life of it, sticking up a station from time to time, or stopping the wagons on the road to the diggings. 'Black Jack of Ballarat' was the name I went under, and our party is still remembered in the colony as *the Ballarat Gang*.

"One day, a gold convoy came down from Ballarat to Melbourne, and we lay in wait for it and attacked it. There were six troopers and six of us, so it was a close thing, but we emptied four of their saddles at the first volley.  Three of our boys were killed, however, before we got the loot.  I put my pistol to the head of the wagon-driver, who was this very man McCarthy.  I wish to the Lord that I had shot him then, but I spared him, though I saw his wicked little eyes fixed on my face, as though to remember every feature.  We got away with the gold, became wealthy men, and made our way over to England without being suspected.  There I parted from my old pals and determined to settle down to a quiet and respectable life.  I bought this estate, which chanced to be in the market, and I set myself to do a little good with my money, to make up for the way in which I had earned it.  I married, too, and though my wife died young she left me my dear little Alice.  Even when she was just a baby, her wee hand seemed to lead me down the right path as nothing else had ever done.  In a word, I turned over a new leaf and did my best to make up for the past.  All was going well ... when McCarthy laid his grip upon me.

"I had gone up to town about an investment, and I met him in Regent Street with hardly a coat to his back or a boot to his foot.

"'Here we are, Jack,' he says, touching me on the arm; 'we'll be as good as a family to you.  There's two of us, me and my son, and you can have the keeping of us.  If you don't—it's a fine, law-abiding country is England, and there's always a policeman within hail.'

"Well, down they came to the west country, there was no shaking them off, and there they have lived rent-free on my best land ever since.  There was no rest for me, no peace, no forgetfulness; turn where I would, there was his cunning, grinning face at my elbow.  It grew worse as Alice grew up, for he soon saw I was more afraid of her knowing my past than of the police. Whatever he wanted he must have, and whatever it was I gave him without question, land, money, houses, until at last he asked a thing which I could not give: He asked for Alice!

"His son, you see, had grown up, and so had my girl, and as I was known to be in weak health, it seemed a fine stroke to him that his lad should step into the whole property. But there I was firm. I would not have his cursed stock mixed with mine; not that I had any dislike to the lad, but his blood was in him, and that was enough! I stood firm. McCarthy threatened. I braved him to do his worst. We were to meet at the pool midway between our houses to talk it over.

"When I went down there, I found him talking with his son, so I smoked a cigar and waited behind a tree until he should be alone. But as I listened to his talk all that was black and bitter in me seemed to come uppermost. He was urging his son to marry my daughter with as little regard for what she might think! It drove me mad to think that I and all that I held most dear should be in the power of such a man as this. Could I not snap the bond? I was already a dying and a desperate man. Though clear of mind and fairly strong of limb, I knew that my own fate was sealed. But my memory and my girl! Both could be saved if I could but silence that foul tongue. I did it, Mr. Holmes. I would do it again. Deeply as I have sinned, I have led a life of martyrdom to atone for it. But that my girl should be entangled in the same meshes which held me was more than I could suffer. I struck him down with no more compunction than if he had been some foul and venomous beast. His cry brought back his son; but I had gained the cover of the wood, though I was forced to go back to fetch the cloak which I had dropped in my flight.

"That is the true story, gentlemen, of all that occurred."

"Well, it is not for me to judge you," said Holmes as the old man signed the statement which had been drawn out. "I pray that we may never be exposed to such a temptation."

"I pray not, sir. And what do you intend to do?"

"In view of your health, nothing. You are yourself aware that you will soon have to answer for your deed at a higher court than the Assizes. I will keep your confession, and if McCarthy is condemned I shall be forced to use it. If not, it shall never be seen by mortal eye; and your secret, whether you be alive or dead, shall be safe with us."

"Farewell, then," said the old man solemnly. "Your own deathbeds, when they come, will be the easier for the thought of the peace which you have given to mine." Tottering and shaking in all his giant frame, he stumbled slowly from the room.

"God help us!" said Holmes after a long silence. "Why does Fate play such tricks with poor, helpless worms? I never hear of such a case as this that I do not think of Baxter's words, and say, 'There, but for the grace of God, goes Sherlock Holmes.'"

James McCarthy was acquitted at the Assizes on the strength of a number of objections which had been drawn out by Holmes and submitted to the defending counsel. Old Turner lived for seven months after our interview, but he is now dead; and there is every prospect that the son and daughter may come to live happily together in ignorance of the black cloud which rests upon their past.

# 5<sup>th</sup> ADVENTURE!
# THE FIVE ORANGE PIPS

When I glance over my notes and records of the Sherlock Holmes cases between the years 1882 and 1890, I am faced by so many which present strange and interesting features that it is no easy matter to know which to choose and which to leave.  Some, however, have already gained publicity through the papers, and others have not offered a field for those peculiar qualities which my friend possessed in so high a degree, and which it is the object of these papers to illustrate.  Some, too, have baffled his analytical skill, and would be, as narratives, beginnings without an ending, while others have been but partially cleared up, and have their explanations founded rather upon conjecture and surmise than on that absolute logical proof which was so dear to him.

There is, however, one of these last which was so remarkable in its details and so startling in its results that I am tempted to give some account of it in spite of the fact that there are points in connection with it which never have been, and probably never will be, entirely cleared up.

The year 1887 furnished us with a long series of cases of greater or less interest, of which I retain the records.  Among my headings under this one twelve months, I find an account of the adventure of the

Paradol Chamber, of the Amateur Mendicant Society, who held a luxurious club in the lower vault of a furniture warehouse, of the facts connected with the loss of the British barque "Sophy Anderson", of the singular adventures of the Grice Patersons in the island of Uffa, and finally of the Camberwell poisoning case.    In the latter, as may be remembered, Sherlock Holmes was able, by winding up the dead man's watch, to prove that it had been wound up two hours before, and that therefore the deceased had gone to bed within that time—a deduction which was of the greatest importance in clearing up the case.

All these I may sketch out at some future date, but none of them present such singular features as the strange train of circumstances which I have now taken up my pen to describe.

It was in the latter days of September, and the seasonal gales had set in with exceptional violence. All day, the wind had screamed and the rain had beaten against the windows, so that even here in the heart of great, hand-made London we were forced to raise our minds for the instant from the routine of life and to recognize the presence of those great elemental forces which shriek at mankind through the bars of his civilization, like untamed beasts in a cage. As evening drew in, the storm grew higher and louder, and the wind cried and sobbed like a child in the chimney.

Sherlock Holmes sat moodily at one side of the fireplace cross-indexing his records of crime, while I at the other was deep in one of Clark Russell's fine sea-stories until the howl of the gale from without seemed to blend with the text, and the splash of the rain to lengthen out into the long swash of the sea waves.  My wife was on a visit to her mother's, and for a few days I was a dweller once more in my old quarters at Baker Street.

"Why," I said, glancing up at my companion, "that was surely the bell.  Who could come tonight?  Some friend of yours, perhaps?"

"Except yourself, I have none," he answered.  "I do not encourage visitors."

"A client, then?"

"If so, it is a serious case.  Nothing less would bring a man out on such a day and at such an hour!  But I take it that it is more likely to be some crony of the landlady's."

Sherlock Holmes was wrong in his conjecture, however, for there came a step in the passage and a tapping at the door.  He stretched out his long arm to turn the lamp away from himself and towards the vacant chair upon which a newcomer must sit.

"Come in!" he said.

The man who entered was young, some twenty-two years at the outside, well-groomed and trimly clad, with something of refinement and delicacy in his bearing.  The streaming umbrella which he held in his hand, and his long shining waterproof coat told of the fierce weather through which he had come.  He looked about him anxiously in the glare of the lamp, and I could see that his face was pale and his eyes heavy, like those of a man who is weighed down with some great anxiety.

"I owe you an apology," he said, raising his golden spectacles to his eyes.  "I trust that I am not intruding.  I fear that I have brought some traces of the storm and rain into your snug chamber."

"Give me your coat and umbrella," said Holmes. "They may rest here on the hook and will be dry presently.  You have come up from the south-west, I see."

"Yes, from Horsham."

"That clay and chalk mixture which I see upon your toe caps is quite distinctive."

"I have come for advice."

"That is easily got."

"And help."

"That is not always so easy."

"I have heard of you, Mr. Holmes.  I heard from Major Prendergast how you saved him in the Tankerville Club scandal."

"Ah, of course.  He was wrongfully accused of cheating at cards."

"He said that you could solve anything."

"He said too much."

"That you are never beaten."

"I have been beaten four times—three times by men, and once by a woman."

"But what is that compared with the number of your successes?"

"It is true that I have been generally successful."

"Then you may be so with me."

"I beg that you will draw your chair up to the fire and favor me with some details as to your case."

"It is no ordinary one."

"None of those which come to me are.  I am the last court of appeal."

"And yet I question, sir, whether, in all your experience, you have ever listened to a more mysterious and inexplicable chain of events than those which have happened in my own family."

"You fill me with interest," Holmes said.  "Please, give us the essential facts from the commencement, and I can afterwards question you as to those details which seem to me to be most important."

The young man pulled his chair up and pushed his wet feet out towards the blaze.

"My name," he said, "is John Openshaw, but my own affairs have, as far as I can understand, little to do with this awful business. It is a hereditary matter; so in order to give you an idea of the facts, I must go back to the commencement of the affair.

"You must know that my grandfather had two sons—my uncle Elias and my father Joseph. My father had a small factory at Coventry, which he enlarged at the time of the invention of bicycling. He was a patentee of the Openshaw unbreakable tire, and his business met with such success that he was able to sell it and to retire upon a handsome competence.

"My uncle Elias emigrated to America when he was a young man and became a planter in Florida, where he was reported to have done very well. At the time of the war, he fought in Jackson's army, and afterwards under Hood, where he rose to be a colonel. When Lee laid down his arms, my uncle returned to his plantation, where he remained for three or four years. About 1869 or 1870, he came back to Europe and took a small estate in Sussex, near Horsham. He had made a very considerable fortune in the States, and his reason for leaving them was his aversion to the negroes, and his dislike of the Republican policy in extending the right to vote to them. He was a singular man, fierce and quick-tempered, very foul-mouthed when he was angry, and of a most retiring disposition. During all the years that he lived at Horsham, I doubt if ever he set foot in the town. He had a garden and two or three fields round his house, and there he would take his exercise, though very often for weeks on end he would never leave his room. He drank a great deal of brandy and smoked very heavily, but he would see no society and did not want any friends, not even his own brother.

"He didn't mind me; in fact, he took a fancy to me, for at the time when he saw me first, I was a youngster of twelve or so. This would be in the year 1878, after he had been eight or nine years in England. He begged my father to let me live with him, and he was very kind to me in his way. When he was sober, he used to be fond of playing backgammon and checkers with me, and he would make me his representative both with the servants and with the tradespeople, so that by the time that I was sixteen I was quite master of the house. I kept all the keys and could go where I liked and do what I liked, so long as I did not disturb him in his privacy. There was one singular exception, however, for he had a single room, a lumber-room up among the attics, which was invariably locked, and which he would never permit either me or anyone else to enter. With a boy's curiosity, I have peeped through the keyhole, but I was never able to see more than such a collection of old trunks and bundles as would be expected in such a room.

"One day—it was in March, 1883—a letter with a foreign stamp lay upon the table in front of the colonel's plate. It was not a common thing for him to receive letters, for his bills were all paid in ready money, and he had no friends of any sort. 'From India!' he said as he took it up, 'Pondicherry postmark! What can this be?' Opening it hurriedly, out there jumped five little dried orange pips, which pattered down upon his plate. I began to laugh at this, but the laugh was struck from my lips at the sight of his face. His lip had fallen, his eyes were protruding, his skin the color of putty, and he glared at the envelope which he still held in his trembling hand, 'K. K. K.!' he shrieked, and then, 'My God, my God, my sins have overtaken me!'

"'What is it, uncle?' I cried.

"'Death,' he said, and rising from the table he retired to his room, leaving me palpitating with horror. I took up the envelope and saw scrawled in red ink upon the inner flap, just above the glue, the letter K three times repeated. There was nothing else save the five dried pips. What could be the reason of his overpowering terror? I left the breakfast-table, and as I ascended the stair I met him coming down with an old rusty key, which must have belonged to the attic, in one hand, and a small brass box, like a cashbox, in the other.

"'They may do what they like, but I'll checkmate them still,' he said with an oath. 'Tell Mary that I shall want a fire in my room today, and send down to Fordham, the Horsham lawyer.'

"I did as he ordered, and when the lawyer arrived I was asked to step up to the room. The fire was burning brightly, and in the grate there was a mass of black, fluffy ashes, as of burned paper, while the brass box stood open and empty beside it. As I glanced at the box I noticed, with a start, that upon the lid was printed the triple K which I had read in the morning upon the envelope.

"'I wish you, John,' my uncle said, 'to witness my will. I leave my estate, with all its advantages and all its disadvantages, to my brother, your father, whence it will, no doubt, descend to you. If you can enjoy it in peace, well and good! If you find you cannot, take my advice, my boy, and leave it to your deadliest enemy. I am sorry to give you such a two-edged thing, but I can't say what turn things are going to take. Kindly sign the paper where Mr. Fordham shows you.'

"I signed the paper as directed, and the lawyer took it away with him. The singular incident made, as you may think, the deepest impression upon me, and I pondered over it and turned it every way in my mind without being able to make anything of it. Yet I could not shake off the vague feeling of dread which it left behind, though the sensation grew less keen as the weeks passed and nothing happened to disturb the usual routine of our lives. I could see a change in my uncle, however. He drank more than ever, and he was less inclined for any sort of society. Most of his time he would spend in his room, with the door locked upon the inside, but sometimes he would emerge in a sort of drunken frenzy and would burst out of the house and tear about the garden with a revolver in his hand, screaming out that he was afraid of no man, and that he was not to be cooped up, like a sheep in a pen, by man or devil. When these hot fits were over, however, he would rush fretfully in at the door and lock and bar it behind him, like a man who can brazen it out no longer against the terror which lies at the roots of his soul. At such times I have seen his face, even on a cold day, glisten with moisture, as though it were new raised from a basin.

"Well, to come to an end of the matter, Mr. Holmes, and not to abuse your patience, there came a night when he made one of those drunken sallies from which he never came back. We found him, when we went to search for him, face downward in a little green-scummed pool, which lay at the foot of the garden.  There was no sign of any violence, and the water was but two feet deep, so that the jury, having regard to his known eccentricity, brought in a verdict of 'suicide.'  But I, who knew how he winced from the very thought of death, had much difficulty in persuading myself that he had gone out of his way to meet it.  The matter passed, however, and my father entered into possession of the estate, and of some 14,000 pounds, which lay to his credit at the bank."

"One moment," Holmes interposed, "your statement is, I foresee, one of the most remarkable to which I have ever listened.  Let me have the date of the reception by your uncle of the letter, and the date of his supposed suicide."

"The letter arrived on March 10, 1883.  His death was seven weeks later, upon the night of May 2nd."

"Thank you.  Please proceed."

"When my father took over the Horsham property, he, at my request, made a careful examination of the attic, which had been always locked up.  We found the brass box there, although its contents had been destroyed.  On the inside of the cover was a paper label, with the initials of K. K. K. repeated upon it, and 'Letters, memoranda, receipts, and a register' written beneath.  These, we presume, indicated the nature of the papers which had been destroyed by Colonel Openshaw.  For the rest, there was nothing of much importance in the attic save a great many scattered papers and notebooks bearing upon my uncle's life in America.  Some of them were of the war time and showed that he had done his duty well and had borne the repute of a brave soldier.  Others were of a date during the reconstruction of the Southern states, and were mostly concerned with politics, for he had evidently taken a strong part in opposing the carpet-bag politicians who had been sent down from the North.

"Well, it was the beginning of 1884 when my father came to live at Horsham, and all went as well as possible with us until the January of 1885. On the fourth day after the new year, I heard my father give a sharp cry of surprise as we sat together at the breakfast table.  There he was, sitting with a newly opened envelope in one hand and five dried orange pips in the outstretched palm of the other one.  He had always laughed at what he called my cock-and-bull story about the colonel, but he looked very scared and puzzled now that the same thing had come upon himself.

"'Why, what on earth does this mean, John?' he stammered.

"My heart had turned to lead.  'It is K. K. K.,' I said.

"He looked inside the envelope.  'So it is,' he cried.  'Here are the very letters.  But what is this written above them?'

"'Put the papers on the sundial,' I read, peeping over his shoulder.

"'What papers?  What sundial?' he asked.

"'The sundial in the garden.  There is no other,' I said; 'but the papers must be those that are destroyed.'

"'Pooh!' he said, gripping hard at his courage. 'We are in a civilized land here, and we can't have foolery of this kind.  Where does the thing come from?'

"'From Dundee,' I answered, glancing at the postmark.

"'Some preposterous practical joke,' he said.

'What have I to do with sundials and papers? I shall take no notice of such nonsense.'

"'You should certainly speak to the police,' I said.

"'And be laughed at for my pains? Nothing of the sort!'

"'Then let me do so?'

"'No, I forbid you! I won't have a fuss made about such nonsense.'

"It was in vain to argue with him, for he was a very obstinate man. I went about, however, with a heart which was full of forebodings.

"On the third day after the coming of the letter, my father went from home to visit an old friend of his, Major Freebody, who is in command of one of the forts upon Portsdown Hill. I was glad that he should go, for it seemed to me that he was farther from danger when he was away from home. In that, however, I was in error. Upon the second day of his absence I received a telegram from the major, imploring me to come at once. My father had fallen over one of the deep chalk-pits which abound in the neighborhood, and was lying senseless, with a shattered skull. I hurried to him, but he passed away without having ever regained consciousness. He had, as it appears, been returning from Fareham in the twilight, and as the country was unknown to him and the chalk-pit unfenced, the jury had no hesitation in bringing in a verdict of 'death from accidental causes.' Carefully, as I examined every fact connected with his death, I was unable to find anything which could suggest the idea of murder. There were no signs of violence, no footmarks, no robbery, no record of strangers having been seen upon the roads. And yet I need not tell you that my mind was far from at ease, and that I was well-nigh certain that some foul plot had been woven round him.

"In this sinister way, I came into my inheritance. You will ask me why I did not dispose of it? I answer, because I was well convinced that our troubles were in some way dependent upon an incident in my uncle's life, and that the danger would be as pressing in one house as in another.

"It was in January, 1885, that my poor father met his end, and two years and eight months have elapsed since then. During that time I have lived happily at Horsham, and I had begun to hope that this curse had passed away from the family, and that it had ended with the last generation. I had begun to take comfort too soon, however; yesterday morning, the blow fell in the very shape in which it had come upon my father."

The young man took from his waistcoat a crumpled envelope, and turning to the table he shook out upon it five little dried orange pips.

"This is the envelope," he continued. "The postmark is London—eastern division. Within are the very words which were upon my father's last message: 'K. K. K.'; and then 'Put the papers on the sundial.'"

"What have you done?" asked Holmes.

"Nothing."

"Nothing?"

"To tell the truth"—he sank his face into his thin, white hands—"I have felt helpless. I have felt like one of those poor rabbits when the snake is writhing towards it. I seem to be in the grasp of some resistless, inexorable evil, which no foresight and no precautions can guard against."

"Tut! tut!" cried Sherlock Holmes. "You must act,

man, or you are lost!  Nothing but energy can save you.  This is no time for despair."

"I have seen the police."

"Ah!"

"But they listened to my story with a smile.  I am convinced that the inspector has formed the opinion that the letters are all practical jokes, and that the deaths of my relations were really accidents, as the jury stated, and were not to be connected with the warnings."

Holmes shook his clenched hands in the air. "Incredible stupidity!" he cried.

"They have, however, allowed me a policeman, who may remain in the house with me."

"Has he come with you tonight?"

"No.  His orders were to stay in the house."

Again Holmes raved in the air.

"Why did you come to me," he cried, "and, above all, why did you not come at once?"

"I did not know.  It was only today that I spoke to Major Prendergast about my troubles and was advised by him to come to you."

"It is really two days since you had the letter.  We should have acted before this.  You have no further evidence, I suppose, than that which you have placed before us—no suggestive detail which might help us?"

"There is one thing," said John Openshaw.  He rummaged in his coat pocket, and, drawing out a piece of discolored, blue-tinted paper, he laid it out upon the table.  "I have some remembrance," he said, "that on the day when my uncle burned the papers I observed that the small, unburned margins which lay amid the ashes were of this particular color. I found this single sheet upon the floor of his room, and I am inclined to think that it may be one of the papers which has, perhaps, fluttered out from among the others, and in that way has escaped destruction. Beyond the mention of pips, I do not see that it helps us much. I think myself that it is a page from some private diary. The writing is undoubtedly my uncle's."

Holmes moved the lamp, and we both bent over the sheet of paper, which showed by its ragged edge that it had indeed been torn from a book. It was headed, "March, 1869," and beneath were the following enigmatical notices:

"4th. Hudson came. Same old platform.

"7th. Set the pips on McCauley, Paramore, and John Swain, of St. Augustine.

"9th. McCauley cleared.

"10th. John Swain cleared.

"12th. Visited Paramore. All well."

"Thank you!" said Holmes, folding up the paper and returning it to our visitor. "And now you must on no account lose another instant. We cannot spare time even to discuss what you have told me. You must get home instantly and act."

"What shall I do?"

"There is but one thing to do—it must be done at once! You must put this piece of paper which you have shown us into the brass box which you have described. You must also put in a note to say that all the other papers were burned by your uncle, and that this is the only one which remains. You must assert that in such words as will carry conviction with them. Having done this, you must at once put the box out upon the sundial, as directed. Do you understand?"

"Entirely."

"Do not think of revenge, or anything of the sort, at present. I think that we may gain that by means of the law; but we have our web to weave, while theirs is already woven. The first consideration is to remove the pressing danger which threatens you. The second is to clear up the mystery and to punish the guilty parties."

"I thank you," said the young man, rising and pulling on his overcoat. "You have given me fresh life and hope. I shall certainly do as you advise."

"Do not lose an instant. And, above all, take care of yourself in the meanwhile, for I do not think that there can be a doubt that you are threatened by a very real and imminent danger. How do you go back?"

"By train from Waterloo."

"It is not yet nine. The streets will be crowded, so I trust that you may be in safety. And yet you cannot guard yourself too closely."

"I am armed."

"That is well. Tomorrow I shall set to work upon your case."

"I shall see you at Horsham, then?"

"No, your secret lies in London. It is there that I shall seek it."

"Then I shall call upon you in a day, or in two days, with news as to the box and the papers. I shall take your advice in every detail." He shook hands with us and took his leave. Outside, the wind still screamed and the rain splashed and pattered against the windows. This strange, wild story seemed to have come to us from amid the mad elements—blown in upon us like a sheet of sea-weed in a gale—and now to have been reabsorbed by them once more.

Sherlock Holmes sat for some time in silence, with his head sunk forward and his eyes bent upon the red glow of the fire.  Then he leaned back.

"I think, Watson," he remarked at last, "that of all our cases, we have had none more fantastic than this."

"Save, perhaps, the Sign of Four."

"Well, yes.  Save, perhaps, that.  And yet this John Openshaw seems to me to be walking amid even greater perils than did the Sholtos."

"But have you," I asked, "formed any definite conception as to what these perils are?"

"There can be no question as to their nature," he answered.

"Then what are they?  Who is this K. K. K., and why does he pursue this unhappy family?"

Sherlock Holmes closed his eyes and placed his elbows upon the arms of his chair, with his finger-tips together.  "The ideal reasoner," he remarked, "would, when he had once been shown a single fact in all its bearings, deduce from it not only all the chain of events which led up to it but also all the results which would follow from it.  As Cuvier could correctly describe a whole animal by the contemplation of a single bone, so the observer who has thoroughly understood one link in a series of incidents should be able to accurately state all the other ones, both before and after.  We have not yet grasped the results which the reason alone can attain to. Problems may be solved in the study which have baffled all those who have sought a solution by the aid of their senses.

"To carry the art, however, to its highest pitch, it is necessary that the reasoner should be able to utilize all the facts which have come to his knowledge; and this in itself implies, as you will readily see, a possession of all knowledge, which, even in these days of free education and encyclopedias, is a somewhat rare accomplishment. It is not so impossible, however, that a man should possess all knowledge which is likely to be useful to him in his work, and this I have endeavored in my case to do. If I remember rightly, you on one occasion, in the early days of our friendship, defined my limits in a very precise fashion."

"Yes," I answered, laughing. "It was a singular document. Philosophy, astronomy, and politics were marked at zero, I remember. Botany variable, geology profound as regards the mud-stains from any region within fifty miles of town, chemistry eccentric, anatomy unsystematic, sensational literature and crime records unique, violin-player, boxer, swordsman, and lawyer. Those, I think, were the main points of my analysis."

Holmes grinned. "Well," he said, "I say now, as I said then, that a man should keep his little brain-attic stocked with all the furniture that he is likely to use, and the rest he can put away in the lumber-room of his library, where he can get it if he wants it. Now, for such a case as the one which has been submitted to us tonight, we need certainly to muster all our resources. Kindly hand me down the letter K of the 'American Encyclopedia' which stands upon the shelf beside you...

"Thank you. Now, let us consider the situation and see what may be deduced from it. In the first place, we may start with a strong presumption that Colonel Openshaw had some very strong reason for leaving America. Men at his time of life do not change all their habits and exchange willingly the charming climate of Florida for the lonely life of an English provincial town. His extreme love of solitude in England suggests the idea that he was in fear of someone or something, so we may assume as a working hypothesis that it was fear of someone or something which drove him from America.  As to what it was he feared, we can only deduce that by considering the formidable letters which were received by himself and his successors.  Did you remark the postmarks of those letters?"

"The first was from Pondicherry, the second from Dundee, and the third from London."

"From East London.  What do you deduce from that?"

"They are all seaports.  That the writer was on board a ship."

"Excellent.  We have already a clue.  There can be no doubt that the probability—the strong probability—is that the writer was on board a ship.  And now let us consider another point:  In the case of Pondicherry, seven weeks elapsed between the threat and its fulfilment, in Dundee it was only some three or four days.  Does that suggest anything?"

"A greater distance to travel."

"But the letter had also a greater distance to come."

"Then I do not see the point."

"There is at least a presumption that the vessel in which the man or men are is a sailing-ship.  It looks as if they always send their singular warning or token before them when starting upon their mission.  You see how quickly the deed followed the sign when it came from Dundee.  If they had come from Pondicherry in a steamer, they would have arrived almost as soon as their letter.  But, as a matter of fact, seven weeks elapsed.  I think that those seven weeks represented the difference between the mail-boat which brought the letter and the sailing vessel which brought the writer."

"It is possible."

"More than that. It is probable. And now you see the deadly urgency of this new case, and why I urged young Openshaw to caution. The blow has always fallen at the end of the time which it would take the senders to travel the distance. But this one comes from London, and therefore we cannot count upon delay."

"Good God!" I cried. "What can it mean, this relentless persecution?"

"The papers which Openshaw carried are obviously of vital importance to the person or persons in the sailing-ship. I think that it is quite clear that there must be more than one of them—a single man could not have carried out two deaths in such a way as to deceive a coroner's jury. There must have been several in it, and they must have been men of resource and determination. Their papers they mean to have, *whoever* may hold them. In this way, you see, K. K. K. ceases to be the initials of an individual and becomes the badge of a society."

"But of what society?"

"Have you never—" said Sherlock Holmes, bending forward and sinking his voice—"have you never heard of the Ku Klux Klan?"

"I never have."

Holmes turned over the leaves of the book upon his knee. "Here it is," he said presently:

"'Ku Klux Klan: A name derived from the fanciful resemblance to the sound produced by cocking a rifle. This terrible secret society was formed by some ex-Confederate soldiers in the Southern states after the Civil War, and it rapidly formed local branches in different parts of the country, notably in Tennessee, Louisiana, the Carolinas, Georgia, and Florida. Its power was used for political purposes, principally for the terrorizing of the negro voters and the murdering and driving from the country of those who were opposed to its views. Its outrages were usually preceded by a warning sent to the marked man in some fantastic but generally recognized shape—a sprig of oak-leaves in some parts, melon seeds or orange pips in others. On receiving this, the victim might either openly abandon his former ways, or might fly from the country. If he braved the matter out, death would unfailingly come upon him, and usually in some strange and unforeseen manner. So perfect was the organization of the society, and so systematic Its methods, that there is hardly a case upon record where any man succeeded in braving it with impunity, or in which any of its outrages were traced home to the perpetrators.

"For some years, the organization flourished in spite of the efforts of the United States government and of the better classes of the community in the South. Eventually, in the year 1869, the movement rather suddenly collapsed, although there have been sporadic outbreaks of the same sort since that date.'

"You will observe," said Holmes, laying down the volume, "that the sudden breaking up of the society was coincident with the disappearance of Openshaw from America with their papers. It may well have been cause and effect. It is no wonder that he and his family have some of the more implacable spirits upon their track. You can understand that this register and diary may implicate some of the first men in the South, and that there may be many who will not sleep easy at night until it is recovered."

"Then the page we have seen—"

"Is such as we might expect. It ran, if I remember right, 'sent the pips to A, B, and C'—that is, sent the society's warning to them. Then there are successive entries that A and B cleared, or left the country, and finally that C was visited, with, I fear, a sinister result for C. Well, I think, Doctor, that we may let some light into this dark place, and I believe that the only chance young Openshaw has in the meantime is to do what I have told him. There is nothing more to be said or to be done tonight, so hand me over my violin and let us try to forget for half an hour the miserable weather and the still more miserable ways of our fellow men."

It had cleared in the morning, and the sun was shining with a subdued brightness through the dim veil which hangs over the great city. Sherlock Holmes was already at breakfast when I came down.

"You will excuse me for not waiting for you," he said; "I have, I foresee, a very busy day before me in looking into this case of young Openshaw's."

"What steps will you take?" I asked.

"It will very much depend upon the results of my first inquiries. I may have to go down to Horsham, after all."

"You will not go there first?"

"No, I shall commence with the City. Just ring the bell and the maid will bring up your coffee."

As I waited, I lifted the unopened newspaper from the table and glanced my eye over it. It rested upon a heading which sent a chill to my heart.

"Holmes," I cried, "you are too late."

"Ah!" he said, laying down his cup, "I feared as much. How was it done?" He spoke calmly, but I could see that he was deeply moved.

"My eye caught the name of Openshaw, and the heading 'Tragedy Near Waterloo Bridge.' Here is the account:

"Between nine and ten last night Police-Constable Cook, of the H Division, on duty near Waterloo Bridge, heard a cry for help and a splash in the water.  The night, however, was extremely dark and stormy, so that, in spite of the help of several passers-by, it was quite impossible to effect a rescue. The alarm, however, was given, and, by the aid of the water-police, the body was eventually recovered. It proved to be that of a young gentleman whose name, as it appears from an envelope which was found in his pocket, was John Openshaw, and whose residence is near Horsham.  It is conjectured that he may have been hurrying down to catch the last train from Waterloo Station, and that in his haste and the extreme darkness he missed his path and walked over the edge of one of the small landing-places for river steamboats.  The body exhibited no traces of violence, and there can be no doubt that the deceased had been the victim of an unfortunate accident, which should have the effect of calling the attention of the authorities to the condition of the riverside landing-stages."

We sat in silence for some minutes, Holmes more depressed and shaken than I had ever seen him.

"That hurts my pride, Watson," he said at last.  "It is a petty feeling, no doubt, but it hurts my pride.  It becomes a personal matter with me now, and, if God sends me health, I shall set my hand upon this gang. That he should come to me for help, and that I should send him away to his death—!" He sprang from his chair and paced about the room in uncontrollable agitation, with a flush upon his sallow cheeks and a nervous clasping and unclasping of his long thin hands.

"They must be cunning devils," he exclaimed at last. "How could they have decoyed him down there? The Embankment is not on the direct line to the station. The bridge, no doubt, was too crowded, even on such a night, for their purpose. Well, Watson, we shall see who will win in the long run. I am going out now!"

"To the police?"

"No; I shall be my own police. When I have spun the web they may take the flies, but not before."

All day I was engaged in my professional work, and it was late in the evening before I returned to Baker Street. Sherlock Holmes had not come back yet. It was nearly ten o'clock before he entered, looking pale and worn. He walked up to the sideboard, and tearing a piece from the bread loaf he devoured it voraciously, washing it down with a long drink of water.

"You are hungry," I remarked.

"Starving. It had escaped my memory. I have had nothing since breakfast."

"Nothing?"

"Not a bite. I had no time to think of it."

"And how have you succeeded?"

"Well."

"You have a clue?"

"I have them in the hollow of my hand. Young Openshaw shall not long remain unavenged. Why, Watson, let us put their own devilish trade-mark upon them. It is well thought of!"

"What do you mean?"

He took an orange from the cupboard, and

tearing it to pieces, he squeezed out the pips upon the table. Of these he took five and thrust them into an envelope. On the inside of the flap he wrote "S. H. for J. O." Then he sealed it and addressed it to "Captain James Calhoun, Barque 'Lone Star,' Savannah, Georgia."

"That will await him when he enters port," he said, chuckling. "It may give him a sleepless night. He will find it as sure a precursor of his fate as Openshaw did before him."

"And who is this Captain Calhoun?"

"The leader of the gang. I shall have the others, but he first."

"How did you trace it, then?"

He took a large sheet of paper from his pocket, all covered with dates and names.

"I have spent the whole day," he said, "over Lloyd's registers and files of the old papers, following the future career of every vessel which touched at Pondicherry in January and February in '83. There were thirty-six ships of fair tonnage which were reported there during those months. Of these, one, the 'Lone Star,' instantly attracted my attention, since, although it was reported as having cleared from London, the name is that which is given to one of the states of the Union."

"Texas, I think."

"I was not and am not sure which; but I knew that the ship must have an American origin."

"What then?"

"I searched the Dundee records, and when I found that the barque 'Lone Star' was there in January, '85, my suspicion became a certainty. I then inquired as to the vessels which lay at present in the port of London."

"Yes?"

"The 'Lone Star' had arrived here last week. I went down to the Albert Dock and found that she had been taken down the river by the early tide this morning, homeward bound to Savannah. I wired to Gravesend and learned that she had passed some time ago, and as the wind is easterly I have no doubt that she is now past the Goodwins and not very far from the Isle of Wight."

"What will you do, then?"

"Oh, I have my hand upon him. He and the two mates are, as I learn, the only native-born Americans in the ship. The others are Finns and Germans. I know, also, that they were all three away from the ship last night. I had it from the dock worker who has been loading their cargo. By the time that their sailing-ship reaches Savannah, the mail-boat will have carried this letter, and the cable will have informed the police of Savannah that these three gentlemen are badly wanted here upon a charge of murder."

There is ever a flaw, however, in the best laid of human plans, and the murderers of John Openshaw were never to receive the orange pips which would show them that another, as cunning and as resolute as themselves, was upon their track. Very long and very severe were the equinoctial gales that year. We waited long for news of the "Lone Star" of Savannah, but none ever reached us. We did at last hear that, somewhere far out in the Atlantic, a shattered stern-post of a boat was seen swinging in the trough of a wave, with the letters "L. S." carved upon it, and that is all which we shall ever know of the fate of the "Lone Star."

# 6<sup>th</sup> ADVENTURE!
# THE MAN WITH THE TWISTED LIP

Isa Whitney, brother of the late Elias Whitney, D.D., Principal of the Theological College of St. George's, was much addicted to opium.  The habit grew upon him, as I understand, from some foolish freak when he was at college; for having read De Quincey's description of his dreams and sensations, he had drenched his tobacco with laudanum in an attempt to produce the same effects.  He found, as so many more have done, that the practice is easier to attain than to get rid of, and for many years he continued to be a slave to the drug, an object of mingled horror and pity to his friends and relatives. I can see him now, with yellow, pasty face, drooping lids, and pin-point pupils, all huddled in a chair, the wreck and ruin of a noble man.

One night—it was in June, 1889—there came a ring to my bell, about the hour when a man gives his first yawn and glances at the clock.  I sat up in my chair, and my wife laid her needle-work down in her lap and made a little face of disappointment.

"A patient!" she said.  "You'll have to go out."

I groaned, for I was newly come back from a weary day.

We heard the door open, a few hurried words, and then quick steps upon the linoleum.  Our own door flew open, and a lady, clad in some dark-colored stuff, with a black veil, entered the room.

"You will excuse my calling so late," she began, and then, suddenly losing her self-control, she ran forward, threw her arms about my wife's neck, and sobbed upon her shoulder. "Oh, I'm in such trouble!" she cried; "I do so want a little help."

"Why," my wife said, pulling up her veil, "it is Kate Whitney!  How you startled me, Kate!  I had no idea who you were when you came in."

"I didn't know what to do, so I came straight to you."  That was always the way.  Folk who were in grief came to my wife like birds to a lighthouse.

"It was very sweet of you to come.  Now, you must have some wine and water, and sit here comfortably and tell us all about it.  Or should you rather that I sent James off to bed?"

"Oh, no, no!  I want the doctor's advice and help, too.  It's about Isa.  He has not been home for two days.  I am so frightened about him!"

It was not the first time that she had spoken to us of her husband's drug trouble—to me as a doctor; to my wife as an old friend and school companion. We soothed and comforted her by such words as we could find.  Did she know where her husband was? Was it possible that we could bring him back to her?

It seems that it was.  She had the surest information that of late he had, when the fit was on him, made use of an opium den in the farthest east of the City.  Until now, his binges had always been confined to one day, and he had come back, twitching and shattered, in the evening.  But now the spell had been upon him forty-eight hours, and he lay there, doubtless among the dregs of the docks, breathing in the poison or sleeping off the effects. There he was to be found, she was sure of it, at the

Bar of Gold, in Upper Swandam Lane. But what was she to do? How could she, a young and timid woman, make her way into such a place and pluck her husband out from among the ruffians who surrounded him?

There was the case, and of course there was but one way out of it. Might I not escort her to this place? And then, as a second thought, why should *she* come at all? I was Isa Whitney's medical adviser, and as such I had influence over him. I could manage it better if I were alone. I promised her on my word that I would send him home in a cab within two hours if he were indeed at the address which she had given me. And so, in ten minutes, I had left my armchair and cheery sitting-room behind me, and was speeding eastward in a hansom cab on a strange errand, as it seemed to me at the time, though the future only could show how strange it was to be.

But there was no great difficulty in the first stage of my adventure. Upper Swandam Lane is a vile alley lurking behind the high wharves which line the north side of the river to the east of London Bridge. Between a slop-shop and a gin-shop, approached by a steep flight of steps leading down to a black gap like the mouth of a cave, I found the den of which I was in search. Ordering my cab to wait, I passed down the steps, worn hollow in the center by the ceaseless tread of drunken feet; and, by the light of a flickering oil-lamp above the door, I found the latch and made my way into a long, low room, thick and heavy with the brown opium smoke, and terraced with wooden berths, like the forecastle of an emigrant ship.

Through the gloom one could dimly catch a

glimpse of bodies lying in strange fantastic poses, bowed shoulders, bent knees, heads thrown back, and chins pointing upward, with here and there a dark, lack-luster eye turned upon the newcomer. Out of the black shadows there glimmered little red circles of light, now bright, now faint, as the burning poison waxed or waned in the bowls of the metal pipes.   Most lay silent, but some muttered to themselves, and others talked together in a strange, low, monotonous voice, their conversation coming in gushes, and then suddenly tailing off into silence, each mumbling out his own thoughts and paying little heed to the words of his neighbor.  At the farther end was a small brazier of burning charcoal, beside which on a three-legged wooden stool there sat a tall, thin old man, with his jaw resting upon his two fists, and his elbows upon his knees, staring into the fire.

As I entered, a sickly Malayan attendant had hurried up with a pipe for me and a supply of the drug, beckoning me to an empty berth.

"Thank you.  I have not come to stay," I said. "There is a friend of mine here—Mr. Isa Whitney—and I wish to speak with him."

There was movement and an exclamation from my right, and peering through the gloom, I saw Whitney, pale, haggard, and unkempt, staring out at me.

"My God!  It's Watson," he said.  He was in a pitiable state of reaction, with every nerve in a twitter. "I say, Watson, what time is it?"

"Nearly eleven."

"Of what day?"

"Of Friday, June 19th."

"Good heavens!  I thought it was Wednesday. It is Wednesday.  What d'you want to frighten a chap for?" He sank his face onto his arms and began to sob in a high treble key.

"I tell you that it is *Friday*, man. Your wife has been waiting two days for you. You should be ashamed of yourself!"

"So I am! But you've got mixed, Watson, for I have only been here a few hours, three pipes, four pipes—I forget how many. But I'll go home with you. I wouldn't frighten Kate—poor little Kate. Give me your hand! Have you a cab?"

"Yes, I have one waiting."

"Then I shall go in it. But I must owe something. Find what I owe, Watson. I am all off color. I can do nothing for myself."

I walked down the narrow passage between the double row of sleepers, holding my breath to keep out the vile, stupefying fumes of the drug, and looking about for the manager. As I passed the tall man who sat by the brazier, I felt a sudden pluck at my skirt, and a low voice whispered, "Walk past me, and then look back at me." The words fell quite distinctly upon my ear. I glanced down. They could only have come from the old man at my side, and yet he sat now as absorbed as ever, very thin, very wrinkled, bent with age, an opium pipe dangling down from between his knees, as though it had dropped in sheer lassitude from his fingers. I took two steps forward and looked back. It took all my self-control to prevent me from breaking out into a cry of astonishment. He had turned his back so that none could see him but I. His form had filled out, his wrinkles were gone, the dull eyes had regained their fire, and there, sitting by the fire and grinning at my surprise, was none other than *Sherlock Holmes*! He made a slight motion to me to approach him, and instantly, as he turned his face half round to the company once more, subsided into a doddering, loose-lipped senility.

"Holmes!" I whispered. "What on earth are you doing in this den?"

"As low as you can," he answered; "I have excellent ears. If you would have the great kindness to get rid of that inebriated friend of yours, I should be exceedingly glad to have a little talk with you."

"I have a cab outside."

"Then please send him home in it. You may safely trust him, for he appears to be too limp to get into any mischief. I should recommend you also to send a note by the cabman to your wife to say that you have thrown in your lot with me. If you will wait outside, I shall be with you in five minutes."

It was difficult to refuse any of Sherlock Holmes' requests, for they were always so exceedingly definite, and put forward with such a quiet air of mastery. I felt, however, that when Whitney was once confined in the cab my mission was practically accomplished; and for the rest, I could not wish anything better than to be associated with my friend in one of those singular adventures which were the normal condition of his existence. In a few minutes I had written my note, paid Whitney's bill, led him out to the cab, and seen him driven through the darkness.

In a very short time, a decrepit figure had emerged from the opium den, and I was walking down the street with Sherlock Holmes. For two streets he shuffled along with a bent back and an uncertain foot. Then, glancing quickly round, he straightened himself out and burst into a hearty fit of laughter.

"I suppose, Watson," he said, "that you imagine that you were certainly surprised to find me there. But not more so than *I* to find *you*."

"I came to find a friend."

"And I to find an *enemy*."

"An enemy?"

"Yes; one of my natural enemies, or, shall I say, my natural prey. Briefly, Watson, I am in the midst of a very remarkable inquiry, and I have hoped to find a clue in the incoherent ramblings of these sots, as I have done before now. Had I been recognized in that den, my life would not have been worth an hour's purchase; for I have used it before now for my own purposes, and the rascally Lascar who runs it has sworn to have vengeance upon me. There is a trapdoor at the back of that building, near the corner of Paul's Wharf, which could tell some strange tales of what has passed through it upon the moonless nights."

"What! You do not mean bodies?"

"Aye, bodies, Watson. We should be rich men if we had 1000 pounds for every poor devil who has been done to death in that den. It is the vilest murder-trap on the whole riverside, and I fear that Neville St. Clair has entered it never to leave it more. But our trap should be here." He put his two forefingers between his teeth and whistled shrilly—a signal which was answered by a similar whistle from the distance, followed shortly by the rattle of wheels and the clink of horses' hoofs.

"Now, Watson," said Holmes, as a tall dogcart dashed up through the gloom, throwing out two golden tunnels of yellow light from its side lanterns. "You'll come with me, won't you?"

"If I can be of use."

"Oh, a trusty comrade is *always* of use; and a chronicler still more so! My room at The Cedars is a double-bedded one."

"The Cedars?"

"Yes; that is Mr. St. Clair's house. I am staying there while I conduct the inquiry."

"Where is it, then?"

"Near Lee, in Kent. We have a seven-mile drive before us."

"But I am all in the dark."

"Of course you are. You'll know all about it presently. Jump up here. All right, John; we shall not need you. Here's half a crown. Look out for me tomorrow, about eleven. So long, then!"

He flicked the horse with his whip, and we dashed away through the endless succession of somber and deserted streets, which widened gradually, until we were flying across a broad balustrade bridge, with the murky river flowing sluggishly beneath us. Beyond lay another dull wilderness of bricks and mortar, its silence broken only by the heavy, regular footfall of the policeman, or the songs and shouts of some belated party of revelers. A dull wrack was drifting slowly across the sky, and a star or two twinkled dimly here and there through the rifts of the clouds.

Holmes drove in silence, with his head sunk upon his breast and the air of a man who is lost in thought, while I sat beside him, curious to learn what this new quest might be which seemed to tax his powers so sorely, and yet afraid to break in upon the current of his thoughts. We had driven several miles, and were beginning to get to the fringe of the belt of suburban villas, when he shook himself and shrugged his shoulders with the air of a man who has satisfied himself that he is acting for the best.

"You have a grand gift of silence, Watson," he said. "It makes you quite invaluable as a companion.

Upon my word, it is a great thing for me to have someone to talk to, for my own thoughts are not overly pleasant. I was wondering what I should say to this dear little woman tonight when she meets me at the door."

"You forget that I know nothing about it."

"I shall just have time to tell you the facts of the case before we get to Lee. It seems absurdly simple, and yet, somehow I can get nothing to go upon. There's plenty of thread, no doubt, but I can't get the end of it into my hand. Now, I'll state the case clearly and concisely to you, Watson, and maybe you can see a spark where all is dark to me."

"Proceed, then."

"Some years ago—to be definite, in May, 1884—there came to Lee a gentleman, Neville St. Clair by name, who appeared to have plenty of money. He took a large villa, laid out the grounds very nicely, and lived generally in good style. By degrees, he made friends in the neighborhood, and in 1887 he married the daughter of a local brewer, by whom he now has two children. He had no occupation, but was invested in several companies and went into town as a rule in the morning, returning by the 5:14 from Cannon Street every night. Mr. St. Clair is now thirty-seven years of age, is a man of temperate habits, a good husband, a very affectionate father, and a man who is popular with all who know him. I may add that his whole debts at the present moment, as far as we have been able to ascertain, amount to 88 pounds, while he has 220 pounds standing to his credit in the Capital and Counties Bank. There is no reason, therefore, to think that money troubles have been weighing upon his mind.

"Last Monday, Mr. Neville St. Clair went into town

rather earlier than usual, remarking before he started that he had two important commissions to perform, and that he would bring his little boy home a box of bricks. Now, by the merest chance, his wife received a telegram upon this same Monday, very shortly after his departure, to the effect that a small parcel of considerable value which she had been expecting was waiting for her at the offices of the Aberdeen Shipping Company. Now, if you are well up in your London, you will know that the office of the company is in Fresno Street, which branches out of Upper Swandam Lane, where you found me tonight. Mrs. St. Clair had her lunch, started for the City, did some shopping, proceeded to the company's office, got her packet, and found herself at exactly 4:35 walking through Swandam Lane on her way back to the station. Have you followed me so far?"

"It is very clear."

"If you remember, Monday was an exceedingly hot day, and Mrs. St. Clair walked slowly, glancing about in the hope of seeing a cab, as she did not like the neighborhood in which she found herself. While she was walking in this way down Swandam Lane, she suddenly heard a cry, and was struck cold to see her husband looking down at her and, as it seemed to her, beckoning to her from a second-floor window. The window was open, and she distinctly saw his face, which she describes as being terribly agitated. He waved his hands frantically to her, and then vanished from the window so suddenly that it seemed to her that he had been plucked back by some irresistible force from behind. One singular point which struck her quick feminine eye was that although he wore some dark coat, such as he had started to town in, he had on neither collar nor necktie.

"Convinced that something was amiss with him, she rushed down the steps—for the house was none other than the opium den in which you found me tonight!—and, running through the front room, she attempted to ascend the stairs.  At the foot of the stairs, however, she met this Lascar scoundrel of whom I have spoken, who thrust her back and, aided by a Dane, who acts as assistant there, pushed her out into the street.  Filled with the most maddening doubts and fears, she rushed down the lane and, by rare good fortune, met in Fresno Street a number of constables with an inspector, all on their way to their beat.  The inspector and two men accompanied her back, and in spite of the continued resistance of the proprietor, they made their way to the room in which Mr. St. Clair had last been seen.  There was no sign of him there.  In fact, in the whole of that floor there was no one to be found save a hideous-looking crippled wretch, who, it seems, made his home there.  Both he and the Lascar stoutly swore that no one else had been in the front room during the afternoon.  So determined was their denial that the inspector was staggered, and had almost come to believe that Mrs. St. Clair had been deluded when, with a cry, she sprang at a small merchandise box which lay upon the table and tore the lid from it.  Out fell a cascade of children's bricks—it was the toy which he had promised to bring home!

"This discovery, and the evident confusion which the cripple showed, made the inspector realize that the matter was serious.  The rooms were carefully examined, and results all pointed to an abominable crime.  The front room was plainly furnished as a sitting-room and led into a small bedroom, which looked out upon the back of one of the wharves.

Between the dock and the bedroom window is a narrow strip, which is dry at low tide but is covered at high tide with at least four and a half feet of water. The bedroom window was a broad one and opened from below.  On examination, traces of blood were seen upon the windowsill, and several scattered drops were visible upon the wooden floor of the bedroom.  Thrust away behind a curtain in the front room were all the clothes of Mr. Neville St. Clair, with the exception of his coat.  His boots, his socks, his hat, and his watch—all were there.  There were no signs of violence upon any of these garments, and there were no other traces of Mr. Neville St. Clair.  He apparently must have gone out of the window, for no other exit could be discovered, and the ominous bloodstains upon the sill gave little promise that he could save himself by swimming, for the tide was at its very highest at the moment of the tragedy.

"And now as to the villains who seemed to be immediately implicated in the matter.  The Lascar was known to be a man of the vilest antecedents, but as, by Mrs. St. Clair's story, he was known to have been at the foot of the stairs within a very few seconds of her husband's appearance at the window, he could hardly have been more than an accessory to the crime.  His defense was one of absolute ignorance, and he protested that he had no knowledge as to the doings of Hugh Boone, his lodger, and that he could not account in any way for the presence of the missing gentleman's clothes.

"So much for the Lascar manager!  Now for the sinister cripple who lives upon the second floor of the opium den, and who was certainly the last human being whose eyes rested upon Neville St. Clair—his name is Hugh Boone, and his hideous face is one which is familiar to every man who goes much to the City. He is a professional beggar, though in order to avoid the police regulations he pretends to a small trade in wax vestas. Some little distance down Threadneedle Street, upon the left-hand side, there is, as you may have remarked, a small angle in the wall. Here it is that this creature takes his daily seat, cross-legged with his tiny stock of matches on his lap, and as he is a piteous spectacle a small rain of charity descends into the greasy leather cap which lies upon the pavement beside him. I have watched the fellow more than once before ever I thought of making his professional acquaintance, and I have been surprised at the harvest which he has reaped in a short time! His appearance, you see, is so remarkable that no one can pass him without observing him—a shock of orange hair, a pale face disfigured by a horrible scar, which, by its contraction, has turned up the outer edge of his upper lip, a bulldog chin, and a pair of very penetrating dark eyes, which present a singular contrast to the color of his hair, all mark him out from amid the common crowd of beggars and so, too, does his wit, for he is ever ready with a reply to any piece of chaff which may be thrown at him by the passers-by. This is the man whom we now learn to have been the lodger at the opium den, and to have been the last man to see the gentleman of whom we are in quest."

"But a cripple!" I said. "What could he have done single-handed against a man in the prime of life?"

"He is a cripple in the sense that he walks with a limp; but in other respects, he appears to be a powerful and well-nurtured man. Surely your medical experience would tell you, Watson, that weakness in one limb is often compensated for by exceptional strength in the others."

"Please, continue your narrative."

"Mrs. St. Clair had fainted at the sight of the blood upon the window, and she was escorted home in a cab by the police, as her presence could be of no help to them in their investigations. Inspector Barton, who had charge of the case, made a very careful examination of the premises, but without finding anything which threw any light upon the matter. One mistake had been made in not arresting Boone instantly, as he was allowed some few minutes during which he might have communicated with his friend the Lascar, but this fault was soon remedied, and he was seized and searched, without anything being found which could incriminate him. There were, it is true, some blood-stains upon his right shirt-sleeve, but he pointed to his ring-finger, which had been cut near the nail, and explained that the bleeding came from there, adding that he had been to the window not long before, and that the stains which had been observed there came doubtless from the same source. He denied strenuously having ever seen Mr. Neville St. Clair and swore that the presence of the clothes in his room was as much a mystery to him as to the police. As to Mrs. St. Clair's assertion that she had actually seen her husband at the window, he declared that she must have been either mad or dreaming. He was removed, loudly protesting, to the police station, while the inspector remained upon the premises in the hope that the ebbing tide might afford some fresh clue.

"And it did, though they hardly found upon the mud-bank what they had feared to find. It was Neville St. Clair's coat, *not* Neville St. Clair, which lay uncovered as the tide receded. And what do you think they found in the pockets?"

"I cannot imagine."

"No, I don't think you would guess. Every pocket stuffed with pennies and half-pennies—421 pennies and 270 half-pennies.  It was no wonder that it had not been swept away by the tide.  But a human body is a different matter.  There is a fierce eddy between the wharf and the house.  It seemed likely enough that the weighted coat had remained when the stripped body had been sucked away into the river."

"But I understand that all the other clothes were found in the room.  Would the body be dressed in a coat alone?"

"No, sir, but the facts might be met superficially enough.  Suppose that this man Boone had thrust Neville St. Clair through the window—there is no human eye which could have seen the deed.  What would he do then?  It would, of course, instantly strike him that he must get rid of the telltale garments.  He would seize the coat, then, and be in the act of throwing it out, when it would occur to him that it would swim and not sink.  He has little time, for he has heard the scuffle downstairs when the wife tried to force her way up, and perhaps he has already heard from his Lascar confederate that the police are hurrying up the street.  There is not an instant to be lost!  He rushes to some secret hoard, where he has accumulated the fruits of his beggary, and he stuffs all the coins upon which he can lay his hands into the pockets to make sure of the coat's sinking.  He throws it out, and would have done the same with the other garments had not he heard the rush of steps below, and only just had time to close the window when the police appeared."

"It certainly sounds feasible."

"Well, we will take it as a working hypothesis for want of a better.  Boone, as I have told you, was arrested and taken to the station, but it could not be shown that there had ever before been anything against him.  He had for years been known as a professional beggar, but his life appeared to have been a very quiet and innocent one.  There the matter stands at present, and the questions which have to be solved—what Neville St. Clair was doing in the opium den, what happened to him when there, where is he now, and what Hugh Boone had to do with his disappearance—are all as far from a solution as ever.  I confess that I cannot recall any case within my experience which looked at the first glance so simple and yet which presented such difficulties!"

While Sherlock Holmes had been detailing this singular series of events, we had been whirling through the outskirts of the great town until the last straggling houses had been left behind, and we rattled along with a country hedge upon either side of us.  Just as he finished, however, we drove through two scattered villages, where a few lights still glimmered in the windows.

"We are on the outskirts of Lee," said my companion.  "We have touched on three English counties in our short drive, starting in Middlesex, passing over an angle of Surrey, and ending in Kent.  See that light among the trees?  That is The Cedars, and beside that lamp sits a woman whose anxious ears have already, I have little doubt, caught the clink of our horse's feet."

"But why are you not conducting the case from Baker Street?" I asked.

"Because there are many inquiries which must be made out here.  Mrs. St. Clair has most kindly put two rooms at my disposal, and you may rest assured that she will have nothing but a welcome for my friend and colleague. I hate to meet her, Watson, when I have no news of her husband. Here we are. Whoa, there, whoa!"

We had pulled up in front of a large villa which stood within its own grounds. A stableboy had run out to the horse's head, and springing down, I followed Holmes up the small, winding gravel drive which led to the house. As we approached, the door flew open, and a little blonde woman stood in the opening, clad in some sort of light muslin of silk, with a touch of fluffy pink chiffon at her neck and wrists. She stood with her figure outlined against the flood of light, one hand upon the door, one half-raised in her eagerness, her body slightly bent, her head and face protruded, with eager eyes and parted lips, a standing question.

"Well?" she cried, "well?" And then, seeing that there were two of us, she gave a cry of hope which sank into a groan as she saw that my companion shook his head and shrugged his shoulders.

"No good news?"

"None."

"But no bad?"

"No."

"Thank God for that! But come in. You must be weary, for you have had a long day."

"This is my friend, Dr. Watson. He has been of most vital use to me in several of my cases, and a lucky chance has made it possible for me to bring him out and associate him with this investigation."

"I am delighted to see you," she said, pressing my hand warmly. "You will, I am sure, forgive anything that may be wanting in our arrangements, when you consider the blow which has come so suddenly upon us."

"My dear madam," I said, "I am an old campaigner, and if I were not I can very well see that no apology is needed. If I can be of any assistance, either to you or to my friend here, I shall be indeed happy."

"Now, Mr. Sherlock Holmes," said the lady as we entered a well-lit diningroom, upon the table of which a cold supper had been laid out, "I should very much like to ask you one or two plain questions, to which I beg that you will give a plain answer."

"Certainly, madam."

"Do not trouble about my feelings. I am not hysterical, nor given to fainting. I simply wish to hear your real, real opinion."

"Upon what point?"

"In your heart of hearts, do you think that Neville is alive?"

Sherlock Holmes seemed to be embarrassed by the question. "Frankly, now!" she repeated, standing upon the rug and looking keenly down at him as he leaned back in a basket chair.

"Frankly, then, madam ... I do not."

"You think that he is dead?"

"I do."

"Murdered?"

"I don't say that. *Perhaps*."

"And on what day did he meet his death?"

"On Monday."

"Then perhaps, Mr. Holmes, you will be good enough to explain how it is that I have received a letter from him today!"

Sherlock Holmes sprang out of his chair as if he had been galvanized.

"What?!" he roared.

"Yes, today." She stood smiling, holding up a little slip of paper in the air.

"May I see it?"

"Certainly."

He snatched it from her in his eagerness, and, smoothing it out upon the table, he drew over the lamp and examined it intently. I had left my chair and was gazing at it over his shoulder. The envelope was a very coarse one and was stamped with the Gravesend postmark and with the date of that very day, or rather of the day before, for it was considerably after midnight.

"Coarse writing," murmured Holmes. "Surely this is not your husband's writing, madam."

"No, but the enclosure is."

"I perceive also that whoever addressed the envelope had to go and inquire as to the address."

"How can you tell that?"

"The name, you see, is in perfectly black ink, which has dried itself. The rest is of the greyish color, which shows that blotting-paper has been used. If it had been written straight off, and then blotted, none would be of a deep black shade. This man has written the name, and there has then been a pause before he wrote the address, which can only mean that he was not familiar with it. It is, of course, a trifle, but there is nothing so important as trifles. Let us now see the letter. Ha! There has been an enclosure here!"

"Yes, there was a ring. His signet ring."

"And you are sure that this is your husband's handwriting?"

"One of his handwritings."

"One?"

"His handwriting when he wrote hurriedly. It is

very unlike his usual writing, and yet I know it well."

"'Dearest, do not be frightened. All will come well. There is a huge error which it may take some little time to rectify.  Wait in patience. —NEVILLE.' Written in pencil upon the fly-leaf of a book, octavo size, no watermark.  Hum!  Posted today in Gravesend by a man with a dirty thumb. Ha! And the flap has been gummed, if I am not very much in error, by a person who had been chewing tobacco.  And you have no doubt that it is your husband's handwriting, madam?"

"*None*.  Neville wrote those words."

"And they were posted today at Gravesend.  Well, Mrs. St. Clair, the clouds lighten, though I should not venture to say that the danger is over."

"But he must be alive, Mr. Holmes!"

"Unless this is a clever forgery to put us on the wrong scent.  The ring, after all, proves nothing.  It may have been taken from him."

"No, no; it *is*, it is his very own writing!"

"Very well.  It may, however, have been written on Monday and only posted today."

"... that is possible."

"If so, much may have happened between."

"Oh, you must not discourage me, Mr. Holmes! I know that all is well with him.  There is so keen a connection between us that I should know if evil came upon him.  On the very day that I saw him last, he cut himself in the bedroom, and yet I, in the diningroom, rushed upstairs instantly with the utmost certainty that something had happened.  Do you think that I would respond to such a trifle and yet be ignorant of his death?"

"I have seen too much not to know that the impression of a woman may be more valuable than the conclusion of an analytical reasoner. And in this letter you certainly have a very strong piece of evidence to corroborate your view. But if your husband is alive and able to write letters, why should he remain away from you?"

"I cannot imagine. It is unthinkable."

"And on Monday he made no remarks before leaving you?"

"No."

"And you were surprised to see him in Swandam Lane?"

"Very much so."

"Was the window open?"

"Yes."

"Then he might have called to you?"

"He might."

"He only, as I understand, gave an inarticulate cry?"

"Yes."

"A call for help, you thought?"

"Yes. He waved his hands."

"But it might have been a cry of surprise. Astonishment at the unexpected sight of you might cause him to throw up his hands?"

"It is possible."

"And you thought he was pulled back?"

"He disappeared so suddenly!"

"He might have leaped back. You did not see anyone else in the room?"

"No, but this horrible man confessed to having been there, and the Lascar was at the foot of the stairs."

"Quite so. Your husband, as far as you could see, had his ordinary clothes on?"

"But without his collar or tie. I distinctly saw his

bare throat."

"Had he ever spoken of Swandam Lane?"

"Never."

"Had he ever showed any signs of having taken opium?"

"Never!"

"Thank you, Mrs. St. Clair. Those are the principal points about which I wished to be absolutely clear. We shall now have a little supper and then retire, for we may have a very busy day tomorrow."

A large and comfortable double-bedded room had been placed at our disposal, and I was quickly between the sheets, for I was weary after my night of adventure. Sherlock Holmes was a man, however, who, when he had an unsolved problem upon his mind, would go for days, and even for a week, without rest, turning it over, rearranging his facts, looking at it from every point of view until he had either fathomed it or convinced himself that his data were insufficient. It was soon evident to me that he was now preparing for an all-night sitting. He took off his coat and waistcoat, put on a large blue robe, and then wandered about the room collecting pillows from his bed and cushions from the sofa and armchairs. With these he constructed a sort of Eastern divan, upon which he perched himself cross-legged. In the dim light of the lamp I saw him sitting there, his eyes fixed vacantly upon the corner of the ceiling, silent, motionless, with the light shining upon his strong-set hooked features. So he sat as I dropped off to sleep, and so he sat when a sudden cry caused me to wake up, and I found the summer sun shining into the apartment.

"Awake, Watson?" he asked.

"Yes."

"Game for a morning drive?"

"Certainly."

"Then dress.  No one is stirring yet, but I know where the stableboy sleeps, and we shall soon have the trap out." He chuckled to himself as he spoke, his eyes twinkled, and he seemed a different man to the somber thinker of the previous night.

As I dressed I glanced at my watch.  It was no wonder that no one was stirring.  It was twenty-five minutes past four!  I had hardly finished when Holmes returned with the news that the boy was putting in the horse.

"I want to test a little theory of mine," he said, pulling on his boots.  "I think, Watson, that you are now standing in the presence of one of the most absolute fools in Europe.  I deserve to be kicked from here to Charing Cross!  But I think I have the key of the affair now."

"And where is it?" I asked, smiling.

"In the bathroom," he answered.  "Oh, yes, I am not joking," he continued, seeing my look of incredulity.  "I have just been there, and I have taken it out, and I have got it in this Gladstone bag.  Come on, my boy, and we shall see whether it will not fit the lock."

We made our way downstairs as quietly as possible, and out into the bright morning sunshine.  In the road stood our horse and trap, with the half-clad stableboy waiting at the head.  We both sprang in, and away we dashed down the London Road.  A few country carts were stirring, bearing in vegetables to the metropolis, but the lines of villas on either side were as silent and lifeless as some city in a dream.

"It has been in some points a singular case," said Holmes, flicking the horse on into a gallop. "I confess that I have been as blind as a mole, but it is better to learn wisdom late than never to learn it at all."

In town the earliest risers were just beginning to look sleepily from their windows as we drove through the streets of the Surrey side. Passing down the Waterloo Bridge Road we crossed over the river, and dashing up Wellington Street wheeled sharply to the right and found ourselves in Bow Street. Sherlock Holmes was well known to the force, and the two constables at the door saluted him. One of them held the horse's head while the other led us in.

"Who is on duty?" asked Holmes.

"Inspector Bradstreet, sir."

"Ah, Bradstreet, how are you?" A tall, stout official had come down the stone-flagged passage, in a peaked cap and frogged jacket. "I wish to have a quiet word with you, Bradstreet."

"Certainly, Mr. Holmes. Step into my room here."

It was a small, office-like room, with a huge ledger upon the table, and a telephone projecting from the wall. The inspector sat down at his desk.

"What can I do for you, Mr. Holmes?"

"I called about that beggarman, Boone—the one who was charged with being concerned in the disappearance of Mr. Neville St. Clair, of Lee."

"Yes. He was brought up and remanded for further inquiries."

"So I heard. You have him here?"

"In the cells."

"Is he quiet?"

"Oh, he gives no trouble. But he is a dirty scoundrel."

"Dirty?"

"Yes, it is all we can do to make him wash his hands, and his face is as black as a potter's. Well, when once his case has been settled, he will have a regular prison bath; and I think, if you saw him, you would agree with me that he needed it."

"I should like to see him very much."

"Would you? That is easily done. Come this way. You can leave your bag."

"No, I think that I'll take it."

"Very good. Come this way, if you please." He led us down a passage, opened a barred door, passed down a winding stair, and brought us to a whitewashed corridor with a line of doors on each side.

"The third on the right is his," said the inspector. "Here it is!" He quietly shot back a panel in the upper part of the door and glanced through.

"He is asleep," he said. "You can see him very well."

We both put our eyes to the grating. The prisoner lay with his face towards us, in a very deep sleep, breathing slowly and heavily. He was a middle-sized man, coarsely clad as became his calling, with a colored shirt protruding through the rent in his tattered coat. He was, as the inspector had said, extremely dirty, but the grime which covered his face could not conceal its repulsive ugliness. A broad welt from an old scar ran right across it from eye to chin, and by its contraction had turned up one side of the upper lip, so that three teeth were exposed in a perpetual snarl. A shock of very bright red hair grew low over his eyes and forehead.

"He's a beauty, isn't he?" said the inspector.

"He certainly needs a wash," remarked Holmes. "I had an idea that he might, and I took the liberty of bringing the tools with me." He opened the Gladstone bag as he spoke, and took out, to my astonishment, a very large bath-sponge.

"He-he!  You are a funny one," chuckled the inspector.

"Now, if you will have the great goodness to open that door very quietly, we will soon make him cut a much more respectable figure."

"Well, I don't know why not," said the inspector. "He doesn't look a credit to the Bow Street cells, does he?"  He slipped his key into the lock, and we all very quietly entered the cell.  The sleeper half-turned, and then settled down once more into a deep slumber. Holmes stooped to the water jug, moistened his sponge, and then rubbed it twice vigorously across and down the prisoner's face.

"Let me introduce you," he shouted, "to Mr. Neville St. Clair, of Lee, in the county of Kent!"

Never in my life have I seen such a sight.  The man's face peeled off under the sponge like the bark from a tree.  Gone was the coarse brown tint!  Gone, too, was the horrid scar which had seamed it across, and the twisted lip which had given the repulsive sneer to the face!  A twitch brought away the tangled red hair, and there, sitting up in his bed, was a pale, sad-faced, refined-looking man, black-haired and smooth-skinned, rubbing his eyes and staring about him with sleepy bewilderment.  Then, suddenly realizing the exposure, he broke into a scream and threw himself down with his face to the pillow.

"Great heavens!" cried the inspector.  "It is, indeed, the missing man!  I know him from the photograph."

The prisoner turned with the reckless air of a man who abandons himself to his destiny. "So be it," he said. "And please, what am I charged with?"

"With making away with Mr. Neville St.— Oh,

come, you can't be charged with that unless they make a case of attempted suicide of it," said the inspector with a grin. "Well, I have been twenty-seven years in the force, but this really takes the cake."

"If I am Mr. Neville St. Clair, then it is obvious that no crime has been committed, and that, therefore, I am illegally detained."

"No crime, but a very great error has been committed," said Holmes.  "You would have done better to have trusted you wife."

"It was not the wife; it was the *children*," groaned the prisoner.  "God help me, I would not have them ashamed of their father. My God! What an exposure! What can I do?"

Sherlock Holmes sat down beside him on the couch and patted him kindly on the shoulder.

"If you leave it to a court of law to clear the matter up," he said, "of course you can hardly avoid publicity. On the other hand, if you convince the police authorities that there is no possible case against you, I do not know that there is any reason that the details should find their way into the papers.  Inspector Bradstreet would, I am sure, make notes upon anything which you might tell us and submit it to the proper authorities. The case would then never go into court at all."

"God bless you!" cried the prisoner passionately. "I would have endured imprisonment—aye, even execution!—rather than have left my miserable secret as a family blot to my children.

"You are the first who have ever heard my story. My father was a schoolmaster in Chesterfield, where I received an excellent education.  I traveled in my youth, took to the stage, and finally became a reporter on an evening paper in London. One day, my editor wished to have a series of articles upon begging in the metropolis, and I volunteered to supply them. There was the point from which all my adventures started. It was only by trying begging as an amateur that I could get the facts upon which to base my articles. When an actor, I had, of course, learned all the secrets of makeup, and had been famous in the greenroom for my skill. I took advantage now of my attainments. I painted my face, and to make myself as pitiable as possible, I made a good scar and fixed one side of my lip in a twist by the aid of a small slip of flesh-colored plaster. Then, with a red head of hair and an appropriate dress, I took my station in the business part of the city, seemingly as a match-seller but really as a beggar. For seven hours I plied my trade, and when I returned home in the evening I found to my surprise that I had received no less than 26 schillings!

"I wrote my articles and thought little more of the matter until, some time later, I backed a bill for a friend and had a writ served upon me for 25 pounds. I was at my wit's end where to get the money, but a sudden idea came to me. I begged a fortnight's grace from the creditor, asked for a holiday from my employers, and spent the time in begging in the City under my disguise. In ten days, I had the money and had paid the debt.

"Well, you can imagine how hard it was to settle down to arduous work at 2 pounds a week when I knew that I could earn as much in a day by smearing my face with a little paint, laying my cap on the ground, and sitting still. It was a long fight between my pride and the money, but the dollars won at last, and I threw up reporting and sat day after day in the corner which I had first chosen, inspiring pity by my ghastly face and filling my pockets with coppers. Only one man knew my secret! He was the keeper of a low den in which I used to lodge in Swandam Lane, where I could every morning emerge as a squalid beggar and in the evenings transform myself into a well-dressed man about town. This fellow, a Lascar, was well paid by me for his rooms, so that I knew that my secret was safe in his possession.

"Well, very soon I found that I was saving considerable sums of money. I do not mean that any beggar in the streets of London could earn 700 pounds a year—which is less than my average takings—but I had exceptional advantages in my power of making up, and also in a facility of repartee, which improved by practice and made me quite a recognized character in the City. All day a stream of pennies, varied by silver, poured in upon me, and it was a very bad day in which I failed to take 2 pounds.

"As I grew richer I grew more ambitious, took a house in the country, and eventually married, without anyone having a suspicion as to my real occupation. My dear wife knew that I had business in the City. She little knew what.

"Last Monday, I had finished for the day and was dressing in my room above the opium den when I looked out of my window and saw, to my horror and astonishment, that my wife was standing in the street, with her eyes fixed full upon me. I gave a cry of surprise, threw up my arms to cover my face, and, rushing to my confidant, the Lascar, entreated him to prevent anyone from coming up to me. I heard her voice downstairs, but I knew that she could not ascend. Swiftly, I threw off my clothes, pulled on those of a beggar, and put on my pigments and wig. Even a wife's eyes could not pierce so complete a disguise. But then it occurred to me that there might be a search in the room, and that the clothes might betray me. I threw open the window, reopening by my violence a small cut which I had inflicted upon myself in the bedroom that morning. Then I seized my coat, which was weighted by the coppers which I had just transferred to it from the leather bag in which I carried my takings. I hurled it out of the window, and it disappeared into the Thames. The other clothes would have followed, but at that moment there was a rush of constables up the stair, and a few minutes after I found, rather, I confess, to my relief, that instead of being identified as Mr. Neville St. Clair, I was arrested as his murderer.

"I do not know that there is anything else for me to explain. I was determined to preserve my disguise as long as possible, and hence my preference for a dirty face. Knowing that my wife would be terribly anxious, I slipped off my ring and confided it to the Lascar at a moment when no constable was watching me, together with a hurried scrawl, telling her that she had no cause to fear."

"That note only reached her yesterday," said Holmes.

"Good God! What a week she must have spent!"

"The police have watched this Lascar," said Inspector Bradstreet, "and I can quite understand that he might find it difficult to post a letter unobserved. Probably he handed it to some sailor customer of his, who forgot all about it for some days."

"That was it," said Holmes, nodding approvingly; "I have no doubt of it. But have you never been prosecuted for begging?"

"Many times; but what was a fine to me?"

"It must stop here, however," said Bradstreet. "If

the police are to hush this thing up, there must be no more of Hugh Boone."

"I have sworn it by the most solemn oaths which a man can take."

"In that case, I think that it is probable that no further steps may be taken. But if you are found again, then all must come out. I am sure, Mr. Holmes, that we are very much indebted to you for having cleared the matter up. I wish I knew how you reach your results."

"I reached this one," said my friend, "by sitting upon five pillows all through the night. I think, Watson, that if we drive to Baker Street, we shall just be in time for breakfast!"

<u>ABOUT THE AUTHOR</u>

Thomas Sewell is a Christian, husband, and father.  He has worked as an editor and journalist, and has won several local awards for his short-stories.

He lives with his family in Chicago, IL.